## *"Why don't you trust me?"*

Quinn's eyes held her gaze intently.

She broke the eye contact and stared at the sunset slowly fading into a night sky. "It's not that easy."

He reached out and covered one of her hands with his. "You can trust me, Jewel."

She pulled her hand out from beneath his, finding his touch far too pleasurable. "You don't know anything about me."

"Then tell me, but hear me. I can't imagine anything that would change my mind about you." His deep voice held a certainty that sent a rush of warmth through her. He moved closer, so close she could smell the scent of his cologne, feel the heat from his body radiating over her. He reached out and touched her lips with his index finger.

"I want you, Jewel, and the only thing that will make me back off is if you tell me that you don't want me."

Dear Reader,

There are times when a book gets written remarkably easily because the characters are so alive and so right for one another. *A Hero of Her Own* was like that. I fell in love with my hero, Quinn, almost immediately. There's nothing more attractive than a man who has the strength to protect, the passion to love and the sensitivity to know just what a woman needs.

When I married my husband, I got that kind of a hero, and after thirty-three years of marriage, he's still the man I want next to me when I go to sleep at night and when I open my eyes in the morning.

My heroine, Jewel, got her hero and I have mine. Here's hoping all my readers find that special man or woman who lights up their world with warmth and love.

Happy reading!

Carla Cassidy

# CARLA CASSIDY

## A Hero of Her Own

Silhouette®

Romantic
SUSPENSE

Special thanks and acknowledgment to
Carla Cassidy for her contribution to the
The Coltons: Family First miniseries.

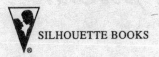

SILHOUETTE BOOKS

Recycling programs
for this product may
not exist in your area.

ISBN-13: 978-0-373-27618-9
ISBN-10:    0-373-27618-4

A HERO OF HER OWN

Visit Silhouette Books at www.eHarlequin.com

Printed in U.S.A.

**Books by Carla Cassidy**

Silhouette Romantic Suspense

*Mustang, Montana
**Sisters
†The Delaney Heirs
††Cherokee Corners
‡Wild West Bodyguards

## CARLA CASSIDY

is an award-winning author who has written more than fifty novels for Silhouette Books. In 1995, she won Best Silhouette Romance from *Romantic Times BOOKreviews* for *Anything for Danny*. In 1998, she also won a Career Achievement Award for Best Innovative Series.

Carla believes the only thing better than curling up with a good book to read is sitting down at the computer with a good story to write. She's looking forward to writing many more books and bringing hours of pleasure to readers.

# Chapter 1

Jewel Mayfair shot up, heart pounding and panic suffocating her with a thick press against her chest. Her bedroom was dark except for the glow from a nightlight plugged into the socket on the wall opposite her bed.

She stared at the light, willing her heartbeat to slow and drawing deep, even breaths to calm down. She'd had the dream again. No, not a dream, it was a nightmare that had plagued her for over two years, ever since the car accident that had taken the life of her fiancé.

Andrew! Her heart cried his name as she remembered the last night they'd had together. Everything had been so perfect. She'd picked him up in her car and they'd gone to their favorite restaurant where he'd surprised her with a proposal, complete with a beautiful ring. And she'd surprised him with some news of her own.

Her hands moved to her flat abdomen. The accident hadn't just taken Andrew from her. It had also taken Andrew's child, who had been growing inside her. Grief pierced her, as rich and raw as it had been when she'd awakened in the hospital after the accident and been told of all that she had lost.

Slowly her breathing returned to normal and she glanced at the clock on her nightstand. Just after midnight. She'd been asleep for less than an hour and she knew from experience that sleep would be a long time coming again.

She slid her long legs over the side of the bed and grabbed the thin robe on the chair nearby. She belted the robe over her short nightgown, then opened the doors that led out of her master bedroom and onto a covered porch.

Despite the hour, the late August heat fell around her like an oppressive veil. Ahead of her was the pool and beyond was the woods that was part of the Hopechest Ranch estate.

In the last six months since coming to Esperanza, Texas, she and the woods had become intimate friends. It was among the tall oaks and thick brush that she spent hours each night when she couldn't sleep. And lately that had been almost every night.

The chlorine scent of the pool hung in the air as

she walked around it to the gate in the back. Opening the gate she paused and looked at the house.

It was still hard for her to believe that she was here in Esperanza, running a ranch for troubled children. The Hopechest Ranch was housed in a beautiful Spanish-style structure made of adobe with a tiled roof.

Jewel had her own quarters and there were four additional bedrooms for the children and a married couple, Jeff and Cheryl Cookson, who were part of the staff.

Seeing no lights on and knowing that if any of the children awakened, the Cooksons would take care of things, she walked out of the gate and into the cooler air beneath the trees.

A light breeze ruffled her short, sun-streaked brown hair as she walked down a well-worn path. She tried to erase from her mind the horrifying visions that haunted her sleep far too often. She was exhausted. Her insomnia was getting worse instead of better.

It was ironic that her job as a psychologist at the ranch was to help children heal from trauma and deal with problems, but for the life of her she couldn't figure out how to heal herself.

She stopped walking and leaned with her back against a huge oak trunk. Closing her eyes, she wondered if she'd ever get a full night's sleep again, if the haunting dreams would ever stop. She'd hoped that by moving from Prosperino, California, she'd leave behind the haunting memories of that accident and her loss. But they'd chased her here and if anything had gotten more intrusive over the last five months.

"Jewel."

Her eyes popped open and she froze, every muscle in her body rigid. Had somebody just uttered her name? Or had it been the wind and an overactive imagination? Her heart banged a more rapid beat as she gazed around her.

The warm night turned icy around her as she cocked her head to listen, narrowed her eyes to see. "Hello?" she said, the word no more than a whisper.

The moonlight was full, spilling down enough light to illuminate the path, but not able to pierce the darkness of the thick woods.

"Jewel."

She gasped. Even though she knew it was impossible, that deep male voice sounded like Andrew's.

"Andrew?" she half whispered his name as tears stung her eyes. She sensed more than saw a form just off to her right. "Andrew, is that you?" Her head filled with wild thoughts.

He hadn't really died in the car accident. It had all been a terrible mixup, a case of mistaken identity. Somehow he'd survived and he'd come here to find her.

"Andrew, wait!" she exclaimed as she saw the shadowy form moving deeper into the woods. Her heart was now pounding so hard it made her half-breathless.

Her mind went blank as she waded through brush and stepped around tree trunks. She had to find him. She was certain the voice she'd heard calling her name was Andrew's. She didn't know how that was possible, didn't care. All she wanted to do was to get to him, to feel his arms around her once again.

Goose bumps rose on her skin and she was half-dizzy as she fought the underbrush, felt the prickly bite of it against her bare legs.

She stumbled into a low-hanging branch. The whack of the limb across her forehead jarred her back to reality. And the reality was that she was in the middle of the woods chasing after a ghost.

The figure she'd been chasing was gone...or had never been there, she thought. Fighting back new tears of despair, she turned and screamed as she bumped into a solid male chest.

"Jewel. It's me. Quinn Logan." His big hands grabbed her shoulders. "Are you all right? I heard you scream."

"I bumped into a tree branch." Her voice sounded far away and she mentally shook herself in an effort to get grounded.

"Come on, let's get back on the path," he said. He dropped his hands from her shoulders, but took one of her hands in his and led her back to the path.

As her mental fog lifted, she jerked her hand from his and stared at him, his handsome features visible in the full moonlight.

He had a mane of brown hair, with flecks of gold and auburn that enhanced his lean features. A scar across one of his cheeks did nothing to detract from his appeal. His topaz eyes glowed feline and, as always when Jewel looked at him, a crazy fluttering went off in her tummy.

"What are you doing out here in the middle of the night, Dr. Logan?" she asked warily. Quinn was the local veterinarian. At six foot three, he had broad shoulders and a quiet simmering energy and strength that made people believe he could handle anything a large animal might do.

"Quinn," he said. "Please make it Quinn, and unfortunately sometimes animals don't get sick during normal business hours. I've been over at Clay's place dealing with a colicky horse." Clay Colton was Jewel's cousin and he lived on the large spread next to the Hopechest Ranch.

"Is the horse all right?" she asked, and wrapped her arms around herself, unable to get back the warmth she'd felt before she'd heard that ghostly voice. Had Quinn been the shape she'd seen in the woods? Had he softly called her name?

"The horse is fine. I'm more concerned about you. You said you hit your head?" He placed two warm fingers beneath her chin and raised her face toward the light. Butterflies went off in her stomach at his touch.

"I'm fine," she said stiffly, and backed away from him.

He reached up and shoved a strand of his hair back from his eyes, gazing at her curiously. "What are you doing out here in the middle of the night?"

She hesitated a moment, then decided to be truthful. "I was having some trouble sleeping and thought maybe a walk outside would help."

"How about I walk you back to your place and see you safely inside?"

"No, thanks. That isn't necessary," she protested. She felt off balance, shocked to find him wandering the woods and still confused by thinking she'd heard somebody call her name.

All she wanted to do was get back to the house and into the safety of her own room. At the moment she felt distinctly unsafe, even though Quinn didn't appear threatening in any way.

"I'll just say good night now," she said. She whirled around and hurried back in the direction of the house, grateful when he didn't try to stop her.

She didn't relax until she was settled in her room with the doors locked. She lingered at the door, peering outside, but there was no sign of anyone—ghosts or otherwise.

Moving away from the door, she took off her robe and climbed back into bed. Her heart still thudded with adrenaline and she knew sleep would be far off, if at all.

She'd gone a little crazy out in the woods, thinking that she heard Andrew's voice calling her, believing for a moment that he was someplace out there in the dark woods.

Or was it possible that Quinn had been playing a cruel game with her? She frowned as she thought of the handsome vet. She'd only run into him a half a dozen times since her arrival in town and usually that was out at Clay's place. But, on each of those occasions, she'd been acutely aware of him, had felt more than a little bit of attraction.

There had been a moment when his warm hands had been on her shoulders when she'd wanted to throw herself against him, feel the heat and strength of his arms enfolding her in an embrace.

She closed her eyes and remembered the sensation of his fingers beneath her chin. It had been so long since a man had touched her in any way. Was it any wonder she'd reacted to his simple touches?

She didn't know what worried her more, the fact that she might be losing her mind or that she was attracted to a man who might, for whatever reason, be playing games with her sanity?

Mornings were chaotic at the Hopechest Ranch and the next morning was no different. The sounds of childish laughter awakened Jewel just after seven and she blessed Cheryl and Jeff Cookson who would be in the kitchen preparing breakfast for the seven children who were currently residents.

The children's ages ranged from ten to thirteen, the eldest a girl who had arrived the previous day from Chicago.

Jewel would have a session with the girl, named Kelsey Cameron, this morning. Jewel had official therapy sessions with each child twice a week, but at the Hopechest Ranch therapy never stopped. Every activity, every conversation provided therapy to heal wounds, buoy self-confidence and get the children on the road to happy, healthy lives.

As Jewel showered and dressed for the day, her mind wandered back to those minutes in the woods with Quinn. Even though she was relatively new to the town, she knew Quinn's story. Clay had told her about how several years ago Quinn had diagnosed one of Clay's horses with a disease that had threatened the rest of the stock. Clay had been forced to put down the prized stud. At the time most of the other local ranchers had thought Quinn's diagnosis was wrong.

Ultimately, Quinn had been vindicated, but not before both his reputation and his practice had taken major hits. Clay had stood by his friend and never missed an opportunity to tell Jewel that Quinn was a great guy.

So what was that great guy doing skulking around the woods last night? If he'd gone to Clay's to take care of a sick horse, why hadn't he driven his truck over instead of making the long trek by foot from his place to Clay's?

Once she left her room, there was no more time for thoughts of Quinn. Breakfast was followed by the counseling session with Kelsey Cameron. The young teenager had come to Hopechest Ranch after four years of being shuttled from family member to family member. Her mother, a drug addict, had just awakened one morning and decided she didn't want to be a mother anymore. One of Kelsey's aunts had contacted Jewel. She was worried about the girl, who had become more angry and withdrawn with each passing day.

Jewel got little from Kelsey, but hadn't expected much in the first session. Besides, today was riding-lesson day, something the children all enjoyed. It was a perfect way for Kelsey to start feeling like a member of their "family."

After lunch, when the children all piled into the minibus, Jewel drove next door to Clay Colton's ranch, the Bar None. As she went the short distance, the kids chattered with excitement, talking about the horses they would ride and Burt Walker, their instructor. She glanced in the rearview mirror and saw that Kelsey sat, staring out the van window, looking as if she'd rather be anywhere else.

The three-hundred-acre Bar None ranch was one of the most successful horse ranches in the area. Clay Colton was one of three illegitimate children of Graham Colton and a pretty rodeo rider named Mary Lynn Grady. Clay was a solid, responsible man and since coming to town Jewel had grown to love him like a brother.

She drove past the two-story ranch house and headed toward the stables. Her stomach did a crazy two-step as she recognized Quinn's black pickup parked nearby. She raised a hand to her hair, momentarily wishing she'd taken more time with it that morning. The thought irritated her and she quickly dropped her hand and parked the bus in front of the stables.

As the children piled out of the bus, Burt walked over to greet them. He was a slender man who'd once been a champion barrel racer. He now worked for Clay and conducted the riding lessons.

"The horses have been waiting for you," he exclaimed to the kids. "They told me last night how much they were looking forward to giving you all a good ride today."

Barry Lundon, a ten-year-old with anxiety issues, widened his eyes. "They talk to you?"

Sam Taylor nudged Barry with his shoulder. "Don't be a baby," he said with his twelve-year-old wisdom. "Horses don't talk."

"Of course they do," Burt said. "They just don't use the same kind of language that we do. Come on, let's get inside and get you all saddled up and I'll tell you about horse language." He winked at Jewel, then led the kids to the second stable.

They'd all just disappeared when Clay, Tamara and Quinn walked out of the building directly in front of her. "I thought I heard the chatter of little voices," Clay said with a warm smile.

"We were just headed to the house for some lemonade," Tamara said. Tamara Brown was Clay's ex-wife. They'd divorced five years ago and she'd become a CSI agent in San Antonio. They'd reunited when a body had been found in a ravine on Clay's ranch and Tamara had been part of the investigating team.

"How are you, Jewel?" Quinn's deep voice evoked memories from the night before when his strong, warm fingers had touched her chin and she'd felt the ridiculous need to jump right into his arms.

"Fine. Just fine," she replied. He looked as attractive this morning as he had the night before in the moonlight. The sun shimmered on his long, thick brown hair finding blond highlights that looked warm and soft. Jewel knew that he was forty-four years old, five years older than she was, but he had an underlying energy that made him seem younger than his years.

"Beautiful day," he said.

"Yes, it's lovely," she replied.

"Before you know it, winter will be here."

Tamara released a tiny sigh of impatience. "You two can stand out here in the heat and talk about the weather until the cows come home. I'm going up to the house for a glass of lemonade." She turned on her heels and headed for the house.

Clay stared after her with the eyes of a man who loved what he saw. *Andrew once looked at me that way,* Jewel thought. She didn't know if she'd ever be ready to pursue a relationship with another man, but she had to admit there were times she missed having somebody look at her that way, as if she were the most important person on the face of the earth.

Clay turned back to face them. "You two coming?"

"I can't," Quinn said as he glanced at his watch. "I've got an appointment in about fifteen minutes.

I've got to get going." Once again he turned his gaze to Jewel. "It was nice seeing you again."

She nodded, those crazy butterflies taking wing in her stomach once again. "You, too."

She and Clay watched as he got into his pickup truck. She was grateful Quinn hadn't mentioned their midnight meeting. She didn't really want Clay to know that she often walked the woods between their places because she suffered nightmares. Her job was healing. She didn't want anyone to find out that she couldn't heal herself.

"He's such a nice guy," Clay said as Quinn's pickup headed down the gravel lane. "And such a talented vet."

"Speaking of vets, I heard you had a horse down last night," she said.

He frowned at her. "A horse down last night? I don't know where you heard that, but it's not true. My stock is all healthy."

He'd lied. Quinn had lied to her the night before. The warmth of the sun on her shoulders couldn't quite warm the chill that suddenly gripped her.

What had Quinn been doing in those woods the night before, and why had he lied?

# Chapter 2

From the moment Jewel had first stepped inside Clay's white wood-frame, two-story home she'd felt the warm welcome it offered. She followed Clay into the wide entry hall and to the rear of the house where a farm-style kitchen opened into a family room.

The family room held two leather couches that faced each other in front of a massive stone fireplace. Western antiques dotted the room, a wagon-wheel coffee table, two lanterns from the 1800s and a framed torn Texas flag that was reported to have flown at the Alamo. The end result was a feeling of old and new, of warmth and permanence.

They didn't go into the family room but instead

stopped in the kitchen, where Tamara had already poured lemonade for them.

"Where's Quinn?" she asked as Clay and Tamara sat at the round oak table.

"He left. He said he had an appointment," Clay explained.

Tamara served their drinks, then joined them at the table. "Did I see a new little face out there this morning?"

Jewel nodded. "Kelsey Cameron. She arrived yesterday from Chicago. Mother a drug addict, father unknown, poor thing has been shuffled from relative to relative for the last four years."

"You'll work your magic, and when she leaves here, she'll have a new sense of self-worth and be wonderfully well-adjusted," Clay said.

Jewel smiled. "You make it sound so easy."

"That's because you make it look easy," Tamara exclaimed. "Your rapport with those kids amazes me."

Jewel waved a hand to dismiss the topic, embarrassed by their praise. "Have you heard that Joe and Meredith are planning a visit?"

Clay leaned back in his chair and nodded. "One of the last stops on the campaign trail."

"I have a feeling the Coltons will be spending Christmases at the White House," Tamara said.

"Uncle President," Clay mused. "Has a nice ring to it."

Jewel laughed. "He's still a few months from winning the presidential election."

"Shouldn't be a problem, especially now that Allan Daniels is out of the running," Clay replied.

Allan Daniels was the current governor of Texas and had been Joe Colton's hottest competition for their party's nomination until his true character had been exposed. Dirty dealing and bribery had effectively neutralized Daniels's threat to Joe's candidacy.

For the next fifteen minutes they talked about the election and how well Joe Colton was doing in the polls. That led to a discussion of politics in general and then the talk turned to more family news.

The Colton family tree was a complicated one. Joe and Meredith had five children of their own and had fostered seven. Jewel's mother, Patsy, who was Meredith's twin sister, had kidnapped Meredith and pretended to be Joe's wife for ten years, giving him three more children. Graham, Joe's brother had two children with his wife, Cynthia, then had indulged in an affair with Mary Lynn Grady and they'd had three children.

Sometimes when Jewel thought about the history of the Colton clan her head hurt, especially when she thought of her own mother, Patsy, who had done horrible things and eventually died in a mental hospital.

Jewel tried not to think of her mother too often. She preferred to think about Charlie and Ruth Baylor, the couple who had adopted her and given her a wonderfully normal Midwestern upbringing. Unfortunately, the couple had since passed away.

"Hello! Anybody home?" The familiar female

voice was followed by the sound of boots against the tile entry floor.

"In the kitchen," Tamara yelled.

Clay's younger sister, Georgie, strode into the kitchen, bringing with her the high energy that was as much a part of her as the waist-length red braid that bobbed down her back. Following at her heels was her husband, Nick Sheffield.

"Georgie, Nick." Clay motioned them toward the table. "Have a seat, we're just enjoying some lemonade and local gossip."

"Hi, Jewel. Saw your kids outside in the corral. Got any future champion riders in the bunch?" Georgie asked. Georgie had spent most of her life on the rodeo circuit as a champion barrel racer. Even the birth of Emmie, her daughter, five years ago hadn't stopped her from competing.

"I don't think so." She laughed. "From what I've seen of them, most are just hanging on to the saddle horn for dear life."

Georgie's green eyes seemed to sparkle with more liveliness than usual as she looked back at her brother. "I've got a surprise for you."

"You know I don't like surprises," Clay returned.

Georgie laughed. "You'll like this one." She turned in the direction of the front door. "Come on in," she yelled.

Jewel's eyes widened as Clay's brother, Ryder, appeared. Next to him was Ana Morales, a Mexican woman who had worked for Jewel before her baby was kidnapped in a black-market ring. Ana held the baby girl in her arms and wore the smile of a woman in love as she gazed up at Ryder.

Clay stood, his face reflecting myriad emotions. Jewel knew the history between the two men, that Ryder's bad-boy lifestyle had led to Clay washing his hands of his younger brother. Jewel knew how painful it had been for Clay to shut his brother out, how tormented he'd been by the difficult decision. But Ryder had turned his life around when he'd been sent to a correctional facility and offered a chance to work undercover for the CIA. He'd cracked open a black-market baby-trafficking operation, saving Ana's little girl and falling in love in the process. During this time, Clay had thought his brother was dead, had grieved for his and the family's loss. Now they had a second chance.

"Hi, Clay," Ryder said, his voice husky with emotion.

There was a moment of charged hesitation, then Clay took two steps forward and embraced his brother. Tears filled Jewel's eyes. Tamara's eyes were suspiciously bright, as well.

Jewel jumped up and hugged Ana. "I've missed you so much," she said. She and Ana had formed a friendship while Ana had worked for her. Jewel cooed over the baby, then stepped back.

It seemed that suddenly everyone was talking at once and in the melee Tamara shocked everyone by confessing that she and Clay had eloped and were married.

As a new round of hugging and backslapping began, Jewel slid out of the room and then out of the house, wanting to leave the family alone for their reunion.

She had a feeling that the issues that had torn Clay and Ryder apart were behind them and the brothers were on their way to building a new, close relationship. She was thrilled for them, but as she walked toward the stables a new sense of loneliness weighed her down.

Clay and Tamara were married and it had been obvious by the glow on Ana's face that she and Ryder were probably not far behind. There seemed to be a marriage epidemic breaking out in Esperanza. But Jewel had not caught the bug, and felt immune to anything even remotely romantic.

On more than one occasion Deputy Adam Rawlings had made it clear that he was interested in pursuing a romantic relationship with her. They'd seen each other socially several times but, try as she might, she just didn't feel more than friendship for him. Besides, with the nightmares she'd been suffering on a regular basis, she was probably better off alone. No man would want to spend his nights with her while she was haunted by ghosts from her past.

She dismissed all thoughts of romance from her mind as she entered the stables. The kids were just finishing up brushing down their horses and Burt approached her with a friendly smile.

"They're just about done," he said.

"How did Kelsey do?" she asked, hoping the new girl had opened up a bit.

"Never said a word to anyone, but she's got a natural seat in the saddle. She grow up around horses?"

"No, just the opposite. She's an inner-city kid, probably has never been on a horse in her life," Jewel replied.

Burt looked over to where Kelsey was working on the horse, a look of fierce concentration on her face. "She shows all the signs of being a born rider. I hope she sticks around long enough for me to work with her more extensively."

"She's not going anywhere for a while. We've got lots of work to do with her," Jewel replied.

It took another half an hour to get all the children loaded into the bus and headed back the short distance to the Hopechest Ranch. The noise level was just below that of a jet engine as they all chatted about their horses and the riding experience. The only one who didn't say a word was Kelsey, who stared out the window as if she were lost in a world of her own.

Jewel was determined to break into that world. It wasn't just her job, it was a calling from her very soul.

"Everybody out and you can have free time play in the garage until dinnertime," Jewel said as she parked in front of the house. One section of the three-car garage had been turned into a playroom, complete with toys and games and craft items.

All the kids headed for the garage except Kelsey, who lingered behind. "Is it okay if I just go to my room?" she asked.

Jewel would have preferred she go with the other children and interact, but she also knew it was going to take some time for Kelsey to feel safe here, to feel as if she were part of the group.

She placed a hand on the girl's shoulder. "That's fine. Dinner is at five-thirty so make sure you're in the kitchen by then."

Kelsey nodded and headed inside. Jewel lingered outside, fighting a wave of exhaustion. The restless nights and bad dreams were getting more frequent, and more difficult to handle.

She raised her face to the warmth of the sun and once again thought about romance. Maybe she was incapable of loving anyone. Maybe the love she'd had for Andrew had been all she had and once it had been given she'd been left empty.

Of course, that didn't explain the odd tingle of excitement she felt whenever she was around Quinn. Female hormones reminding her that she was alive— that's all it was, she told herself.

It was impossible for her to fall in love again, especially with her past visiting her every night in the form of nightmares.

Voices in the night. Visions in the woods. Equally as haunting as the dreams was the fear that somehow she was slowly falling into the mental illness that had consumed her mother.

* * *

"She should be just fine," Quinn assured Ralph Smith, a local rancher who had called him about a cow who had gotten caught in some barbed wire. "All the wounds are superficial and now that I've cleaned her up and applied antibiotic cream, she shouldn't have any problems."

He slapped the rear of the big animal and with a low moo she headed back toward the pasture. "I'd definitely do something about that barbed wire."

Ralph frowned toward a stand of trees and brush. "I didn't even know it was there, just tangled up in all the weeds, but I'll get it out of here today."

Together the two men walked toward the gate in the fence. Initially, coming out here and meeting up with Ralph had been awkward. Ralph had been one of the loudest, most critical ranchers when Quinn had been forced to put down Clay Colton's prized stud.

It had been the second-darkest time in Quinn's life. The darkest had been when he'd lost his wife, Sarah, to cancer.

Even though Quinn had been proven right in his diagnosis of the disease that had infected Clay's stud, even thought his decision to put the horse down had probably saved the rest of the stock, Quinn had never quite gotten over how quickly some of the locals had turned on him.

The fact that Ralph had called him to come and check out the cow was an olive branch he had extended to Quinn. It had been a long time coming, but Quinn wasn't a man to hold a grudge. Life was too damned short.

"Just let me know if the wounds begin to ooze or look infected and I'll come back out," Quinn said as he reached the door of his pickup truck.

"I appreciate it, Doc." Ralph held out his hand and the two men shook.

Minutes later as Quinn drove away from the Smith ranch and back toward town, he thought about those dark days when many in the town had turned their backs on him, made darker because he was still grieving for his wife. At the time all he had was his work and when that took a hit, he considered packing up and leaving Esperanza.

Instead, with the support of the Coltons, Clay in particular, he'd stayed and held his head high. When his decision to put the stud down had been vindicated, he'd put the whole ordeal behind him and got on with his life.

As he drove down Main Street, he decided to stop for dinner at Miss Sue's Café, where he took many of his evening meals. He told himself it was because he hated to cook, but the truth was he dreaded the evening hours spent alone.

An old-fashioned cowbell heralded his arrival as he entered the quaint café. "You're a bit early today, Quinn," Becky French, the owner of the establishment, greeted him with a warm smile.

He smiled at the short, plump woman. "It's never

too early for a good meal." He walked over to one of
the wooden tables by the window and sat in a chair
where he could easily see out the window.

"Got some new pictures," Becky said as she
poured him a cup of coffee. There was nothing Becky
loved more than to show off pictures of her grand-
children. She set the coffeepot down and dug into her
apron pocket to withdraw a handful of photos.

Quinn took them from her and studied each of the
smiling childish faces. "They're beautiful," he said.

Becky smiled and nodded. "They are." She
tucked the photos back in her apron. "I'll just give
you a few minutes. The special is smothered steak
and mashed potatoes."

"Then I don't need a minute. That sounds good."
He returned the menu and leaned back in the chair
to sip his coffee. She scurried away, the gray bun on
top of her head bobbing with her brisk walk.

Kids. At one time Quinn had hoped to have a
house full, but fate and cancer had stolen that
dream from him. He and Sarah had never had a
chance for children.

Even though it was early, there were already other
diners in the café. Quinn had never been in the place
when there weren't at least a handful of people. Most
mealtimes the place was packed.

He'd just finished his coffee when Georgie Sheffield, her husband, Nick, and her daughter, little
Emmie, came through the door.

"I hear we just missed you this morning at Clay's,"

Georgie said to him. "We had a reunion. Ryder and Ana are back in town and we took them to Clay's." Georgie's green eyes sparkled brightly. "It was wonderful."

Emmie sidled up next to Quinn. At five years old, the little girl was the spitting image of her mother. Her red hair was cut pixielike to frame her face and she was dressed just like her mama in jeans, a Western-style shirt and cowboy boots.

Emmie was bright and precocious and had spent most of her young life on the rodeo circuit with her mother. The little girl considered Quinn a special friend because he fixed horses when they got sick and there were few things Emmie loved more than horses and cowboys.

"Excuse me, Mommy, but I want to talk to Mr. Quinn," Emmie said. Georgie smiled with amusement and nodded. "Guess what happens next week?"

"I can't imagine. What?" Quinn replied.

She leaned closer, bringing with her the scent of sunshine and childhood. "School begins."

"Ah." Quinn smiled at her. "And what are you, in the second grade, the third?"

"Maybe I should be because you know I can already read," Emmie exclaimed. She leaned even closer. "But, truly it's going to be my very first day of kindergarten." A fierce look of determination crossed her petite features. "And I'm going to make one new friend, even if he or she isn't a cowboy."

"I think that sounds like a wonderful plan," Quinn said.

Emmie turned to her mother and Nick. "And now I'll go pick us out a table."

As she left the adults behind, Georgie offered Quinn a weak smile. "I can't believe she's starting school. She's so comfortable around adults. Her friends have always been rodeo cowboys. I just hope she fits in okay." Her eyes clouded and sparkled with sudden tears of worry.

"I'm sure she'll be just fine," Quinn said.

"Of course she will," Nick agreed, and placed an arm around Georgie's shoulder. "She's as strong as her mother and almost as pretty."

Georgie laughed and leaned into Nick. He grinned at Quinn. "You just wait, maybe someday you'll have to live through the trauma of the first day of school."

As the two of them joined Emmie, who had chosen a table toward the back of the café, Quinn thought about what Nick had said.

He and Sarah had talked about having children one day, but before that dream had been realized she'd been diagnosed with the malignant aggressive brain tumor that had taken her in six short months. They'd had only nine months of marriage before her diagnosis.

Sarah had been a quiet, thoughtful woman and when she died, she did so as quietly and unassumingly as she had lived. He'd grieved deep and hard for a long time. Now when he thought of Sarah, the sharp despair was gone and he was left with a loneliness and a growing desire to get on with his life.

"Here we are," Becky said as she delivered his

meal. "Anything else I can do for you?" she asked as she poured him another cup of coffee.

"No, thanks. I'm good."

"You're not good," Becky replied, her blue eyes sparkling with the liveliness that was her trademark. "You know I'm not happy unless I'm minding everyone's business but my own. You need a woman, Quinn. You spend far too much time at this table all alone—no offense."

He laughed. "None taken. I was just sitting here thinking the same thing."

"We've got a lot of nice single women in this town who'd love to see you socially. You're that strong, silent type. A little bit of that is quite romantic, but too much of it puts off the ladies."

"I'll keep that in mind," Quinn replied. It was impossible to be offended by Becky's advice because he knew how well intentioned it was.

As she left his table, his thoughts turned to the woman he'd met in the woods the night before. Jewel. From the moment he'd first met her, she'd intrigued him.

Certainly he found her amazingly attractive with her short, tousled, streaked golden-brown hair and big brown eyes. Although slender, she had curves in all the right places and legs that seemed to go on forever.

Last night wasn't the first time he'd seen her wandering the woods around the Hopechest Ranch, although it was the first time he'd let her know he was there.

Quinn had a feeling he and Jewel suffered from the same afflictions—insomnia and loneliness. Quinn often spent the nighttime hours at Clay's place where he boarded his horse, Noches.

What he didn't understand was what had made Jewel scream in the woods the night before and why she'd looked positively haunted when he'd encountered her.

# Chapter 3

As the purple shadows of twilight began to deepen, a responding tension filled Jewel. It wasn't natural for the coming of night to bring something that tasted very much like suppressed terror into the back of her throat.

Jeff and Cheryl were in the process of getting the kids ready for bed and Jewel sat at the kitchen table making a list of school supplies she needed to purchase before school began next week.

When she finished her list, she would tuck each of the children in for the night. Those minutes just before bedtime, when she connected with each of the children with a good-night kiss and a wish for sweet dreams, was an important part of the routine of love that abounded at the ranch.

A knock sounded on the front door and she looked at the clock. Although it felt much later, it was only just after seven.

She hurried to the front door and opened it to see Deputy Adam Rawlings. As usual not a strand of his dark brown hair was out of place and he was impeccably dressed in his khaki uniform. "Hi, Adam."

"I was just out making rounds and thought I'd stop by and say hello," he said.

Jewel flipped on the outside light and stepped out on the porch to join him. "Quiet night?" she asked.

"Most of them are quiet," he replied. "Not that I'm complaining. I heard you've got a new boarder. How's that working out?"

She nodded. "A thirteen-year-old girl named Kelsey from Chicago. If you'd asked me yesterday how things were going I would have said not well. She was quiet and withdrawn. But today she appears more open. She loved the riding lessons at Clay's yesterday and wanted to know when we'd be going again." She broke off as she realized she was beginning to ramble.

"How's everything else going?" he asked. His gaze narrowed slightly. "You look tired."

"I am," she admitted. "I was just sitting at the table, thinking about everything I need to buy for the kids to start school next week." She smiled. "Trying to figure out school supplies for seven kids in seven different classes is enough to make anyone tired."

"I'll let you get back to it. I just thought I'd check

in and see how you were doing." He shifted his muscular body from one foot to the other. "If you get a minute to yourself and want to get dinner out or maybe see a movie, you know all you have to do is just call me."

She smiled. "Thank you, Adam. I'll keep that in mind."

They said goodbye and then she watched as he left the porch and walked back to his patrol car. He seemed like such a nice man, good-looking and obviously interested in her. Unfortunately, she just didn't feel anything for him except a mild friendship.

As his car pulled away, she went back inside to the kitchen table. She finished making her list and by then it was time to kiss the kids good-night.

She went into the boys' bedroom first. The room held two bunk beds and at the moment all four sleeping places were occupied. Barry and Sam, the two older boys, had the top bunks and eight-year-old Jimmy Nigel and seven-year-old Caleb Torrel had the lower bunks.

"All tucked in?" she asked Barry as she approached him first.

He nodded. "Will you keep the nightlight on?" he asked anxiously. "I'm not scared or anything, but I just don't like the dark."

Jewel smiled at the dark-eyed boy. They had this same conversation every night. "The nightlight will be on until morning. Sleep tight, Barry."

As she moved from Barry to Sam and then to the

two younger boys, she couldn't help but think of the baby she'd lost. She'd desperately wanted to be a mother, had been thrilled to discover she was pregnant. The minute the doctor had confirmed what she'd suspected, her heart had filled with a happiness she'd never known before and hadn't known since.

As she moved from the boys' room to the girls', she shoved away thoughts of the baby she'd lost and dreams of what might have been.

There were three girls in residence at the moment. Kelsey slept on the top bunk of one of the beds and on the lower bunks were Lindy Walker and Carrie Lyndon, both ten years old.

Jewel went to Kelsey first. She didn't touch the girl in any way, wouldn't invade Kelsey's personal space unless she was invited to do so. "Ready to call it a night?"

Kelsey nodded, her green eyes less guarded than they'd been the day before. "I'm not used to going to bed so early."

Jewel smiled. "We believe in the routine of early to bed, early to rise around here. Besides, with school starting next week, it's important that all of you get plenty of sleep."

Jewel moved to the other beds, where the girls demanded good-night kisses and hugs, then she left the room and turned out the light. As in the boys' room, a small nightlight burned in a wall socket.

She met Cheryl in the hallway and smiled tiredly. "Another day done," she said.

Cheryl returned her smile and swept a strand of her long, dark hair behind an ear. "I wanted to run an idea by you. Jeff and I would like to plan a day trip for the kids in the next couple of weeks. There's a Native American museum two hours from here and we thought it would be fun to visit the museum and have a picnic lunch at a nearby park."

"Sounds like something they would enjoy," Jewel replied.

"We haven't finalized a day yet, I just wanted to put a bug in your ear about it."

"Let me know what you and Jeff decide and we'll work out the details."

Cheryl nodded. "Then I'll just say good night."

As Cheryl headed toward the front bedroom where she and Jeff slept, Jewel returned to the kitchen. She tucked into her purse the list of supplies she needed to buy, then once again sat at the table to make notes in the files she kept on each of the children.

Busywork. In the back of her mind she knew that's what she was doing, creating work to keep her mind off the fact that soon it would be time to go to bed.

To sleep.

To dream.

Again the taste of dread mingled with a simmering terror. If only she could have one night of peaceful sleep and happy dreams. If only she could wake up in the morning well-rested and happy.

If only Andrew hadn't died in the car accident.

She sighed and focused back on the files in front

of her. These were her children, the ones who came to Hopechest Ranch in need of stability and love. They were all she needed. And maybe a good night's sleep was vastly overrated.

She didn't know how long she'd sat working when she heard a strange scratching sound. She got up from the table and followed the noise to the front door. Definitely sounded like something scratching for attention.

Equally curious and wary, she unlocked the door and cracked it open. The door shoved inward and a chocolate-colored dog jumped up at her. In surprise she stumbled backward and fell on her behind. The dog licked her face as if she were a long-lost friend that he was thrilled to see again.

"Okay, okay," she said with a burst of laughter as the dog continued to lavish her with kisses. She looked up to see Quinn standing in the doorway. Her heart jumped with a quickened beat.

He stepped inside and took the dog by the collar. "Sorry about that," he said as she quickly got to her feet. "He's a Lab and just a puppy so he hasn't learned his manners yet."

"It's okay." Jewel reached up and self-consciously raked her fingers through her hair. As always the sight of Quinn sent an electrical tingle through her. "He's a cutie. Is he yours?"

"Actually, I was hoping he'd be yours," Quinn said.

"Mine?" She looked at him in surprise.

The dog sat on the floor next to him, looking first

at Quinn, then at Jewel, as if aware that they were talking about him.

"It might be presumptuous of me, but I thought maybe you could use a companion, especially when you decide to take a walk in the woods late at night." Quinn shoved a strand of his thick, wavy hair away from his eyes, and shifted from foot to foot, as if suddenly extremely uncomfortable. "Maybe it was a stupid idea."

"No, it was a lovely idea," she replied, touched by the thoughtfulness of the gesture. "Actually, we've talked about getting a dog since I first opened the doors here, but we've just never gotten around to it. What's his name?"

"He doesn't have an official name yet." Quinn's eyes were a warm topaz. "I have to warn you, he's only twelve weeks old. He's not quite housebroken, but he's a big lover and has a terrific personality. Most important, he's great with kids."

"Then how can I possibly turn away such a wonderful gift?" she replied. The children would be positively thrilled with this new addition to the family. "Maybe we'll put him in the garage for tonight. Do you think that's okay?"

He nodded and clipped a leash to the collar. "I'm sure that's fine. Why don't you take him and I'll unload the supplies from the truck."

"Supplies?"

He smiled, a warm, beautiful gesture that detracted from the scar across his cheek and transformed him from slightly dangerous-looking to more than slightly wonderful-looking. "In the truck I've got a doggie bed, food and water bowls, a couple of toys and several bags of kibble."

"Quinn, you didn't have to do all that," she protested as she took the leash from him.

"It wouldn't be fair to give you a gift that cost you a ton of money," he replied. "And along with the gift comes free veterinary services for the life of that guy. Consider it my donation to Hopechest Ranch."

She started to protest once again at the generosity of the gift, but then changed her mind and smiled. "Thank you."

Together they walked out of the door. She headed for one of the three garages as he went out to his truck. The first garage was the playroom for the kids. The second was where she parked her car and the third was currently empty. It was to the empty one that she led the puppy.

As she waited for Quinn she crouched down and stroked the puppy's back. "We'll let the kids give you a name," she said. He gazed at her with big, brown, adoring eyes.

Her heart expanded with warmth. Quinn had brought her a dog to walk in the woods. It was one of the most thoughtful things anyone had ever done for her. He thought she could use a companion.

Had he sensed the deep, abiding loneliness that had been her constant companion for the last couple of years? A loneliness that never went away, no mat-

ter how many people surrounded her, no matter how
the children filled her days and nights.

She stood as he approached with two big sacks of
dog food over his shoulder. Although he was tall and
lean, he had broad, strong shoulders that easily managed the heavy bags.

"I can't believe you did this," she said. As he drew
closer, a new spark of electricity swept through her.

"I figured maybe if you're grateful enough you
might invite me in for a cup of coffee." He set the
bags on the garage floor.

"I think maybe we can work something out," she
replied. She told herself that the crazy buzz she felt
at the very idea of spending some time with him was
nothing more than the pleasure of having somebody
fill these hours of darkness before she finally called
it a night.

It took him only minutes to unload all the items
from his truck. She got the pooch settled for the night,
then Quinn followed her inside and to the kitchen.

The kitchen was one of the largest rooms in the
house, but as Quinn took a seat at the long wooden
table, she felt as if the room shrank. He possessed a
simmering energy beneath his calm, cool exterior, an
energy that seemed to shimmer in the air around him.

"I'm not keeping you up, am I?" he asked as she
made the coffee. "I didn't realize how late it had gotten until I got to your front door."

"It's not a problem," she assured him. "I normally
don't go to bed too early." It was only when she

turned away from him to check on the coffee that she remembered what had happened the night before— their encounter in the woods and the lie he'd told her about what he'd been doing there.

Quinn wasn't sure what happened, but one minute her brown eyes were warm and inviting and the next minute they chilled and held a new wariness.

"You lied to me last night," she said. "You told me that you had been over at Clay's because he had a horse down, but I asked him about it and he said all his stock was healthy."

So that's what had caused the change in her expression. She'd obviously just remembered what he'd told her the night before.

"Yeah, I lied," he admitted. "It was a stupid thing to do. I was embarrassed that I'd bumped into you, embarrassed to tell you the truth."

She remained standing by the counter next to the coffeepot. The coffee was finished brewing but she made no move to get cups. He had a feeling that she was waiting for his explanation and if she didn't like it, then the offer of coffee would be rescinded.

And he didn't want that. It had taken him all evening to work up the nerve to come here. In fact, it had taken him months to work up his nerve to be here. He wanted to have coffee with her. He wanted to know more about her.

"And what, exactly, is the truth?" she asked, the coolness in her voice strong enough to frost his face.

"I don't sleep well, haven't for years. On the nights when I know I won't be able to sleep I go to Clay's and spend time with my horse, Noches. I board him there and right now he's my favorite nighttime companion."

She searched his face, as if on his features she'd discover if he was telling her the truth or not. "Jewel, why else would I be out in the woods in the middle of the night?" he asked.

She turned her back on him to reach for two cups in the overhead cabinet, but not before he saw a flash of emotion in her eyes, an emotion that looked something like fear. "You should have just told me that last night," she replied. She poured the coffee then joined him at the table.

"I haven't been eager for it to get around that the town vet suffers from insomnia. The first time an animal dies for whatever reason everyone will say it's my fault because I don't get enough sleep," he said.

She took a sip of her coffee, her brown eyes gazing at him curiously over the rim of her cup. "It must have been difficult for you," she said as she placed the cup back on the table. "When you had to put down Clay's horse and so many in the town turned against you. Clay told me all about it."

"It was difficult," he agreed, "but it's over and done with, and I try to keep difficult things from my past firmly in the past." As thoughts of Sarah drifted through his mind, he decided a change of topic was in order. "I understand I missed a big reunion over at Clay's place this morning."

"You did." A smile curved her lips and Quinn felt the beauty of the gesture in a starburst of warmth in the pit of his stomach. "It was wonderful to see Clay and Ryder together again. Finally, I think they're going to have the relationship they both want."

Quinn nodded. "I know how badly Ryder's lifestyle hurt Clay, the bad choices his brother made when he was younger, but it sounds like he's turned it all around."

"How did you hear about it—the reunion, I mean?" she asked curiously.

"I ran into Georgie and Nick and Emmie at the café this evening." He smiled. "Emmie told me she's excited to start school next week and she's determined to make one friend who isn't a cowboy."

Jewel laughed and again Quinn's stomach filled with a welcome warmth. She had a nice laugh. "That one is a pip," she said. "I know Georgie has been worried about her fitting in at school. Emmie has spent her whole life on the rodeo circuit with adults as her peers, but I keep telling Georgie that Emmie is going to be just fine. She's so bright, she shouldn't have any problems."

There followed several long moments of uncomfortable silence. Quinn felt like a teenage boy on a first date as he desperately searched for an interesting topic of conversation. He'd been wanting to get to know her better ever since she'd come to town, but it had been years since he'd done the dating dance.

"I'll bet your kids…" he began.

"How did you get…" she said at the same time.

"Go ahead," he said.

"I was just going to ask where you got the dog."

"I helped deliver a litter of four and the owner insisted I get pick of the litter for helping out. I already have a dog and so figured I'd just try to find him a good home. I think this will be a great place for him."

She smiled. "The kids will love him and taking care of him will be therapeutic for them."

He leaned back in his chair, some of his tension beginning to ebb. "You like what you do here."

She nodded, her golden-brown hair sparkling beneath the artificial light. "I love it. I was working for Meredith Colton at the Hopechest Ranch in Prosperino, California, and when she offered me the opportunity to come here and open up a ranch, I jumped at the chance."

"Was it a tough change? Moving here from California?" He took a drink of the coffee.

"Not really. I was ready for a change and, of course, Clay has been very supportive."

"He thinks a lot of you," Quinn said.

"He thinks a lot of you, too."

"He's been a good friend and a great support over the years." Quinn took another sip of his coffee.

"You know, I have the same problem you do with insomnia," she said. She wrapped her slender fingers around her coffee cup and looked more vulnerable than she had moments before. "I start dreading the coming of night just after dinner."

He wasn't surprised by her confession. "Have you seen a doctor? Maybe you could get a prescription for some sleeping medication."

She waved one of her hands. "I don't want to do that. I don't want to medicate myself to sleep. What about you? Have you seen a doctor, Doctor?" she asked lightly.

"No, I'm like you. Eventually after a couple nights of restlessness I manage to get in enough sleep to keep going." He hesitated a moment, then added, "From what Clay has told me, that's not the only thing we have in common."

"What else do we have in common?" One of her eyebrows danced up quizzically.

"We've both lost people we cared deeply about. Clay told me about your fiancé. I'm sorry for your loss."

Her eyes darkened as her complexion paled. "Thank you. It was a tragedy, but it's in the past."

It was obvious by the tightening of her lips, the paleness of her skin, that even though it was in her past, she still felt deeply the grief of the loss. She cleared her throat. "What about you? Who did you lose?"

"My wife, Sarah."

"I'm sorry. I didn't realize you'd been married." Some of the color returned to her cheeks.

"We weren't married long before she was diagnosed with a brain tumor. Six months later she was gone."

To his surprise Jewel reached out and covered his hand with hers. "Oh, Quinn. I'm so sorry."

Her touch sizzled through him and he turned his hand over so that he now grasped her hand. "The only reason I told you this is because I want you to know that I understand grief, that if you need somebody to talk to, I have a good ear and strong shoulders."

She pulled her hand from his as if suddenly uncomfortable by the physical connection. "I appreciate the offer, but I'm doing okay. Tell me about Sarah. What was she like?"

"Quiet and sweet. We met while I was in school. I was getting my degree in veterinary medicine and she wanted to be a nurse. It began as friendship and grew into love. She loved animals almost as much as I did and we talked about having a dozen kids and twice as many dogs and cats. What about your fiancé, Andy…wasn't that his name?"

"Andrew, never Andy," she replied, her eyes going soft. "He owned an accounting firm. He loved numbers and puzzles and he'd asked me to be his wife on the night that he died."

"Clay told me it was a car accident."

She nodded and once again wrapped her fingers around her cup, as if seeking warmth from the coffee it still contained. "We were driving home from the restaurant where we'd eaten dinner. It was misting and the road was dark. A Hummer seemed to come out of nowhere and steered right into the driver side of our car. I was knocked unconscious." One of her hands moved to splay on her stomach. "The driver of the Hummer was never found."

Quinn wanted to reach out to her, to pull her into his arms and hold her until her haunted, vulnerable look went away. "Even though you can't ever prepare yourself for the death of somebody you love, I had six months to prepare myself for saying goodbye to Sarah, but you had no time to prepare yourself for saying goodbye to Andrew."

She shrugged. "It happened. It's over and life moves on." She glanced at the clock on the stove.

"It's getting late," he said, taking it as a hint. "I should get out of here." She didn't argue and he stood and carried his cup to the sink. "Thanks for the coffee," he said as they walked to the front door.

"Thanks for the dog," she replied. "It was a very thoughtful thing for you to do." She opened the front door and leaned against it.

He knew she was waiting for him to walk out, but he was reluctant to leave. "Jewel, I'm sorry if our conversation brought back bad memories." He'd finally gotten an opportunity to talk to her one-on-one and the topic of conversation he'd chosen was their painful pasts.

To his horror her eyes misted with tears. "I'm sorry," she said as the tears spilled onto her cheeks.

He stepped toward her then, unable to stand by while she cried, feeling guilty because he was responsible for her tears. He should have talked about the weather, or about town politics, about anything but loss.

He opened his arms to her and to his surprise she walked into them and laid her head against his chest.

He embraced her, the scent of her soft, floral perfume eddying in the air.

The last thing he'd expected when he'd arrived here tonight was to have her in his arms, but when she raised her face to look up at him, he knew he wanted to take it one step further. He desperately wanted to kiss her.

*Chapter 4*

Jewel knew he was going to kiss her. His intent shone hot in his amazingly gorgeous eyes. In the back of her mind she knew this was crazy, that she didn't know this man well enough to kiss him and she certainly wasn't interested in a relationship of any kind.

Still, that rational part of her brain was no match for the wave of sharp, visceral desire that swept through her as she gazed up at him. She parted her lips as he dipped his head to take her mouth with his.

Crazy. It was pure madness that possessed her, but she gave in to it. His mouth was hot, the kiss sending a shaft of warmth up and down her veins. She welcomed the feeling, welcomed him as she opened her mouth more to him, allowing him to deepen the kiss with his tongue.

She knew she should step back and call a halt to things, but it had been so long and Quinn's arms were so strong around her and his kiss made her ache for more.

His hands stroked the length of her back as his mouth continued to ply hers with fire. She wrapped her arms around his neck and tangled her fingers in his soft, sexy mane of hair.

She swirled her tongue with his, felt her knees weaken and threaten to buckle. She clung to him more tightly, her heart beating a rhythm of desire.

His mouth finally left hers and moved down the length of her neck, nipping and teasing with slow, deliberate intent. She dropped her head back, allowing him to kiss her throat, and trail his hot mouth along her collarbone.

It didn't matter that she'd only known him on a casual, social level until now. She didn't care that this was probably one of the most foolish things she'd ever done. For right now, in his arms, she wanted to be foolish and abandon herself to being held by Quinn, being kissed by Quinn.

Once again his mouth captured hers and as she pressed more tightly against him she realized that he was aroused. This knowledge only made her desire flame higher.

She wanted to make love with him. She wanted

to lose herself in his caresses, in the very mindless sensations of sex.

She'd heard enough about Quinn from Clay to know he wouldn't hurt her, that she was safe with him. She wasn't concerned about consequences. The most she'd have to worry about was perhaps a little embarrassment the morning after. But she didn't care about the morning after—all she cared about was here and now.

"Miss Jewel?"

Jewel and Quinn shot apart like two guilty teenagers at the sound of the young voice drifting down the hallway. Jewel recognized the voice. She drew a deep breath to steady herself, not looking at Quinn. "Lindy, what's wrong?"

"You'd better come quick, Kelsey is packing her suitcase and says she's gonna run away."

"I'll be right there." Jewel finally looked at Quinn as she felt the heat of a blush warm her cheeks. Okay, so her embarrassment hadn't waited until the morning after.

"You need help?" he asked softly.

"No, I'll be fine. Please, just go." Now that the heat of the moment had passed, she was appalled by what had just happened between them…what had almost happened between them.

She was grateful that he didn't argue but simply nodded and left. She closed the front door behind him then hurried down the hallway to the girls' room where Kelsey was throwing her clothes into the battered cloth suitcase she'd arrived with.

"Kelsey, what's going on?" Jewel asked.

The girl didn't stop her activity and kept her eyes downcast. "Nothing. I just don't want to be here anymore."

"Has something happened? Did somebody say something to upset you?" Jewel took a step closer to the young teenager.

"No. I just gotta go, that's all. I've got to leave." She glanced up at Jewel, tears filling her bright green eyes.

Jewel stepped toward her and held out her hand. "Come on, let's go someplace where you and I can have a little private chat."

Kelsey hesitated a moment, then slipped her hand into Jewel's. "Lindy, Carrie, back to bed and lights out," she said as she led Kelsey from the room.

She took the girl into the kitchen and gestured her to the chair where Quinn had sat. "Want a glass of milk? Maybe a cookie?"

Kelsey shook her head, her face radiating abject misery. Jewel sat in the chair next to Kelsey's and took the girl's cold, small hands into hers. "Honey, I can't help you if you don't talk to me," she said softly.

Kelsey caught her lower lip in her teeth, then released it and sighed. "I like it here. That's the whole problem."

"I'm sorry. I don't understand," Jewel replied.

Kelsey frowned. "Every time I get someplace where I like to be, then somebody makes me leave. I figured this time I wouldn't wait around for somebody to kick me out. I'd just go, before I like it so much that it hurts to leave."

A sob escaped her. "What's the point of staying here and being happy when I know sometime I'll have to leave and won't be happy again?" she cried.

Jewel leaned forward and gathered the girl into her arms. "I never turn up my nose at happiness," Jewel replied as she stroked Kelsey's hair. "What you have to do with it is grab it and hold it as close as you can for as long as you can. Then when it's gone you have special memories to help you through the bad times. Besides, one of the things we want to do while you're here is teach you some skills so that you can learn to be happy wherever you are."

Kelsey raised her head and looked at her through tear-glazed eyes. "I'm afraid to be happy because it hurts so much when it goes away."

Jewel held her close, her heart aching for the girl. "I know, honey. But I'd like you to stay here with us and grab on to all the happiness we can give you. Let's not talk about when you leave. Heavens, you've only been here for one day."

Kelsey laughed as Jewel released her. "I really don't want to leave," she admitted. "I want to ride the horses some more and I like the other kids, too."

"Good, then how about we get you back into bed? There are a bunch of activities on the schedule for tomorrow and you don't want to start the day tired. You can unpack your things in the morning."

Kelsey nodded and together they walked back to

the girls' room. "Good night," Kelsey said. Jewel watched as she moved her suitcase off the bed and then climbed into the bunk.

With the crisis handled, Jewel returned to the kitchen where she turned out the lights then headed for her own quarters.

Her head filled with a vision of Quinn, and she couldn't believe what had happened between them before he'd left, couldn't imagine what might have happened if they hadn't been interrupted.

Or maybe the problem was she *could* imagine all too well what might have happened. Her mouth heated as she remembered the kisses they'd shared. In another minute she would have led him to her bedroom, allowed him—no, encouraged him—to make love to her.

God, was she so desperate, so lonely that she'd just fall into bed with anyone? She entered the dressing room and stripped off her jeans and T-shirt and threw them into the hamper, then stood in front of the wall mirror and stared at her reflection.

She raked her fingers through her short sunstreaked brown hair and frowned as she saw the tired lines that radiated outward from her eyes.

No, she wasn't desperate enough to fall into bed with any man who showed an interest in her. If that were the case, she would have slept with Deputy Adam Rawlings by now. He'd certainly make it clear he was interested in a romance with her, but she had never wanted to kiss him. Not like she'd wanted to kiss Quinn.

It was Quinn who stirred her like no man had for a very long time. She turned away from the mirror and reached for her nightgown. From the moment she'd first seen him, something about him had drawn her not only on a physical level, but on an emotional level, as well.

There was a solid gentleness about him that attracted her and nothing he'd done this evening had changed her mind. Still, she was a bit embarrassed by how quickly she'd responded to him.

Clad in her nightgown, she went into her bedroom and pulled down the covers on the bed, surprised to realize she not only felt tired, she felt sleepy.

Maybe the conversation with Quinn had relaxed something inside her, or maybe it had just been his calm, steady presence that had created an unusual sense of peace inside her.

She crawled into bed and glanced at the clock on her nightstand. Almost eleven o'clock. Maybe tonight she could actually sleep. She turned out the light on her nightstand, then closed her eyes.

A vision of Quinn at the table filled her mind, his topaz eyes shining with an inner strength, his mouth curved up into a gentle smile. Almost immediately she felt the heaviness of sleep overtaking her and she gave in to it.

The dream began almost immediately. She and Andrew were seated in the restaurant. It was their favorite place to eat, an Italian café with traditional checkered tablecloths and candles in the center of each table. The food was impeccable and the atmosphere conducive to romance.

They had just finished eating when Andrew smiled at her, his blue eyes holding suppressed excitement. "I've spent the entire day today trying to figure out a wonderfully romantic way to do this, but I'm an accountant at heart and that means I'm not very creative." He reached into his shirt pocket and withdrew a ring box.

It was magic. The man, the ring and the moment. The scene shimmered in a golden haze as it played out in her dream. The engagement ring sparkled as he reached for her hand and slid it onto her finger.

And the magic only grew stronger, brighter when she told Andrew her secret, that she was pregnant with his baby. Andrew had been thrilled and they'd excitedly talked about wedding plans and baby names. They'd laughed as they'd left the restaurant.

"Here, baby, you drive," she'd said, and handed him the keys to her car. She'd picked him up at his office and driven to the restaurant. "That way, I can sit and admire my new ring," she's said with a laugh.

The scene shifted abruptly, as dreams often do, and they were in her car, Andrew behind the wheel. The golden light that had shimmered was gone and everything was in the sharp colors of harsh reality.

Even in sleep Jewel knew what was coming and she fought to wake up, not wanting to see the images. But the dreamscape held her captive and she saw the

Hummer appear out of nowhere, a bright yellow monster with sharp silver gnashing teeth.

"No!" she cried, but the monster didn't listen. She watched in horror as those scissor-sharp teeth slammed into their car, then snatched Andrew and shook him like a rag doll.

As the monster tossed Andrew aside, it came for her, biting into her stomach, killing her baby, killing her dreams.

Her screams woke her. She shot straight up in the bed, her heart stuttering so fast in her chest she thought she was going to die. Deep sobs wrenched through her, making it difficult to breathe.

She grabbed her stomach, as if to protect, to save, but she knew it was a futile gesture. The monster had won. He'd managed to take everything away from her, leaving her empty inside.

She remained in the center of her bed, shivering and silently weeping as the nightmare lingered in her head. Why hadn't the driver of the Hummer stopped? Why hadn't he tried to help?

If medical help had been summoned immediately, would Andrew have been saved? Would her baby have lived? These were haunting questions with no answers.

Finally, tears spent, she reached over and turned on her nightlight, knowing that it would be a very long time before she fell asleep again.

She rolled to the side of the bed to get up, and frowned as she heard the crinkle of paper. Puzzled, she slid over and spied what looked like a page from a newspaper.

She picked it up and stared at the headline: Tragic Accident Kills Accounting Executive. She dropped it as if it burned her fingers. It was the original article that had appeared in the paper years ago when the accident had happened.

Her heartbeat, which had finally slowed to a normal pace, now crashed and banged so painfully she couldn't catch her breath. How had the article gotten in her room, in her bed?

Somebody had been in her room. Had someone crept in while she was sleeping? Earlier in the night while she and Quinn had been in the kitchen?

Was he still here now?

She jumped off the bed and grabbed the baseball bat that leaned against the wall in the corner of the room. She didn't want to alarm anyone else in the house, but she needed to make certain that nobody was here who didn't belong here.

Heart pounding so loudly she could hear it in her head, she went back into her quarters, flipping on the lights in the dressing room, the bathroom, then her bedroom. She checked closets and behind doorways. When she'd cleared her quarters, she went through the rest of the house. She checked all the doors and windows, but found nothing out of place and nobody there who didn't belong. The doors and windows were locked tight and showed no breach of any kind.

She finally crept back to her bed. It was just after

one. There would be no more sleep for tonight. She sat with the baseball bat clutched in her hands, and waited for morning to come.


"Rover," Barry exclaimed. "That's a good name for a dog."

"That's a dumb name," Sam replied. "We should call him Champion or Bruno. Those are good dog names."

They were all in the kitchen, where the dog was running from child to child, his tail wagging with happiness. He lavished kisses on everyone he met and Jewel wasn't sure who was happier—the dog or the children.

"He looks like a cup of hot cocoa," Kelsey said.

"That a good name—Cocoa." Carrie clapped her hands. "Here, Cocoa." The dog ran to her and nearly knocked her down.

"I think Cocoa is a wonderful name," Jewel said. Her eyes felt gritty from her lack of sleep and the fear that had gripped her when she'd seen the newspaper article on the bed still simmered just beneath the surface of her consciousness.

"And now what we need to do is divide up the responsibility of taking care of Cocoa," she said, trying to stay focused.

As the kids talked about who would be responsible for feeding and providing fresh water for him, and who would take the dog out for walks, Jewel's thoughts once again returned to the night before.

It had been just before dawn that the idea of something other than a mysterious intruder struck her. On the top shelf in her closet was a cardboard memory box. Inside it were family photos and memorabilia from her past.

She'd had several copies of the newspaper article inside the box. While she had no way of confirming that the copy that had been on her bed had come from her box, she suspected that it might have.

Maybe she'd gotten up in the middle of her nightmare and had taken the article from the box and laid it on the bed. She wasn't sure what frightened her more—the idea of an intruder whose motive apparently was to torment her, or the possibility that she was unconsciously haunting herself.

Was this the way it had begun with her mother? Was this how true madness began? She remembered reading an article in a psychology magazine once about a woman who believed she was being stalked. She received threatening notes in the mail, her car tires were slashed. One incident after another plagued her and the truth was only discovered after her family hired a private investigator. The truth was that she was doing it all to herself with no conscious knowledge of her actions.

"Can we walk him now?" Barry's voice intruded into her disturbing thoughts.

"There's a leash for his collar out in the garage. Sam, why don't you run out and get it, then you can all take turns walking him in the front yard," Jewel said.

As Sam went off to retrieve the leash, Jewel

looked at Cheryl. "I've got some things to do in town today. It's possible I'll be gone most of the day."

"Not a problem. Jeff and I can keep things running smoothly here on the home front," she replied.

"Don't forget that at two today Mark Potter is coming to give an art lesson." Jewel had hired a local artist to come twice a week to give the kids art lessons. She believed in the therapeutic quality of art.

Sam returned with the leash and within minutes all the kids were out in the yard with Cocoa and under the supervision of Jeff.

Jewel went to her bedroom and grabbed her purse, then left the house and got into her car. She waved as she drove down the driveway and smiled as she saw Cocoa, with an exuberant leap, knock Carrie on her behind. Carrie laughed and wrapped her arms around the dog.

The dog had been a great gift from Quinn. Quinn. As she headed toward town, the handsome vet filled her thoughts.

She knew what his mouth tasted like, had felt the silky softness of his amazing hair and his strong shoulders beneath her fingertips. But she didn't know where he came from, what kind of family he had or even what kind of food he liked.

The whole kiss thing had been crazy and as she thought of seeing him again she wasn't sure if the thrum of nerves that tingled inside her was dread or anticipation.

She dismissed him from her mind as she pulled

into a parking space in front of the town library. At some point in the early morning hours, with sleep deprivation weighing heavy, she'd wondered if maybe her unconscious mind was trying to tell her something important, something about the accident that had taken everything she loved away from her.

In those dark predawn hours, she'd realized there was a lot about Andrew and his work she hadn't known. There had always been a small part of her that had believed the accident wasn't an accident at all. The Hummer hadn't attempted to swerve to avoid hitting them. The driver hadn't jammed on the brakes or taken any action to prevent the accident.

Although the authorities had ruled it an accident, due to the mist that had made the country road a bit slick, Jewel had never completely embraced the notion that it had been nothing more than a tragic accident.

She could have done some research on the computer at the ranch, but for some reason she'd felt it was important to keep this separate from her life there. One of the library computers would do just fine for a little research into Andrew's business.

As she entered the library, she was surprised to see sixteen-year-old Sarah Engleleit behind the counter. The teenager had spent some time at the Hopechest Ranch two months ago when she'd run away from home.

"Sarah," she exclaimed. "I didn't know you were working here."

"I just started last week. It's just part-time but I really like it. How are things at the ranch?"

"Busy, as usual." Jewel smiled. "I'm just going to use one of the computers for a while. I'll see you later."

Jewel made her way to one of the computer stations, a new burst of nerves attacking her as she realized she was about to go backward in time, back to where dreams held possibility and the horror of having that possibility stolen away.

For a moment she sat in the chair and fought the impulse to rub her eyes, knowing they were already red enough for somebody to mistake her for a vampire.

She couldn't remember the last time she'd felt so exhausted. It was as if all the nights of insomnia had finally caught up with her this morning, making concentration difficult.

Long and Casey Accounting had been a powerhouse in the business world in California. Andrew had owned the firm and Gray Casey had been a junior partner. When Andrew died, his younger brother stepped into the position Andrew had held and the company had continued to thrive.

The first thing she researched was the accident. There had been several news articles about the tragedy in the days following the wreck.

She tried to maintain an emotional distance as she read over the articles that had been in the local papers, but she learned nothing new from the printed accounts.

By keying in the search words *Long and Casey*

*Accounting* she got over two hundred results. The morning turned to afternoon as she checked each one, unsure what she was looking for, but compelled to continue. She took notes of things she thought might mean something.

It was three o'clock when Sarah came over to where Jewel sat. "I'm leaving and just wanted to say goodbye," she said.

Jewel got up and gave her a hug. "You know you're welcome out at the ranch anytime."

"I know. Maybe one day after school I'll drop by for a visit."

"I'd like that," Jewel replied. As Sarah headed out the front door, Jewel returned to her reading. Her eyes, which had burned earlier, now felt raw.

She was just about to give up the search when she hit an article that caused her to sit up straighter in her chair.

Successful Entrepreneur Indicted for Tax Evasion, the headline read. She scanned the page, wondering why a news report about a James Corrs had been brought up by her typing in Andrew's firm's name. She found her answer on the second page of the article. It had been Andrew who had turned in James Corrs to the Internal Revenue Service.

The date on the newspaper was three weeks before the car accident that had taken Andrew's life. Could this James Corrs have sought revenge against Andrew? Certainly he'd had a lot to lose by battling a tax-evasion charge.

Dear God, was it possible the car accident hadn't been an accident at all, but rather a murder?

As a firm hand fell on her shoulder, a scream of surprise escaped her.

## Chapter 5

"**I**'m sorry, I didn't mean to startle you," Quinn said as he took a step closer to Jewel.

She hurriedly closed the folder in front of her and hit the button to return the computer to the home page. It was as if she didn't want him to see what she'd been doing. "I didn't mean to yell," she replied. "I was just so engrossed that I didn't see you there."

"Engrossed in what?" he asked lightly. She looked both beautiful and terrible. She wore a pair of jeans and a sleeveless blue blouse, but it wasn't her clothes that captured his attention. It was her eyes. They were so red they looked as though, if she opened them wide enough, they'd start to bleed. That, coupled with her drawn, exhausted look, had him worried about her.

"Just a dry psychology article," she replied. Her

gaze didn't quite meet his. "What about you? What are you doing here?"

He held up two books and tried not to think about the searing kiss they'd shared the night before. "I ordered a couple of books from the library in San Antonio and they came in this morning."

"Must be interesting material for you to order it all the way from San Antonio," she replied. She looked nervous, on edge as she clutched the file folder to her chest.

He smiled. "Yeah, *Animal Husbandry and New Medicine for Old Health Problems in Animals.* If I try to read them before I go to bed, they just might solve my insomnia problem."

She laughed, but even that sounded stressed and tired. "I've tried reading before bedtime to get sleepy, but it doesn't work for me." She released a small sigh as she set the folder down on the desk. "Lately, nothing seems to be working for me."

"Ah, but I'll bet you haven't read *Animal Husbandry.* You want to go get a drink?" The invitation sprang from his lips almost before his brain had formed the intention.

She looked so miserable and he was reluctant to just say goodbye, turn and walk away from her.

To his surprise, she hesitated only a moment then nodded. "Actually, a drink sounds great." She got up from the computer station and grabbed her folder from the table. "Where do you want to go?"

"There's a new Mexican place down a block on Main. It's got a nice little bar inside. It's called Joe's Cantina."

She frowned, the gesture emphasizing the tired lines across her forehead. "I haven't heard of it before."

"It's only been open about two weeks. I checked it out last week. The margaritas were great and the food was terrific."

"Okay, sounds good to me," she agreed.

"If you want, we could walk from here."

A moment later they walked out into the late-afternoon sunshine. Quinn dropped off his books in his truck and she put her folder in her car, then together they headed down the sidewalk toward the restaurant.

"Did everything go okay after I left last night?" he asked. "The girl who was going to run away? Did you get her settled down?"

"She didn't really want to run away," she replied. "Poor thing was just scared because she likes the ranch and she didn't want to get attached and have to leave. She's afraid to be happy because she knows what it feels like to have happiness vanish."

"That's a tough thing to know so young."

Jewel nodded, the sunshine catching and sparking on the gold highlights in her hair. "It's tragic. That's the problem with most of the kids who come to the ranch. They've already experienced things that no child should have to go through. Oh, by the way, the dog now has a name. Cocoa."

"Nice," he replied. "So the kids were happy with him?"

She smiled. "Happy is an understatement. They were overjoyed."

"I'm glad. I know Cocoa will be happy there."

As they reached the door to the restaurant the scent of salsa, tortillas and spicy meat filled the air. Quinn opened the door for her, then followed her into the establishment.

On the right side was the seating area for diners and on the left was an intimate bar with small round tables and low lighting. They settled at one of the bar tables and both ordered margaritas.

"I usually don't drink before dinner," she said, as if it were important that he understand that. "And until last night I've never kissed a man who brought me a dog." Her cheeks flamed pink.

Quinn's blood heated as he thought of that kiss. It had taken him a long time and an icy shower after he'd left her ranch to cool down and given the opportunity to kiss her again, he wouldn't hesitate. Even now the thought of kissing her again created a ball of tension in the pit of his stomach.

"Jewel, if you're worried that somehow I think you're a fast woman because of what happened last night, put that worry out of your head. Neither of us planned for it to happen. It just happened, but I'd be less than honest if I didn't tell you that I wouldn't mind if it happened again."

She was saved from having to respond by the waitress, who delivered their drinks and a basket of chips with a bowl of salsa.

"You mentioned last night that you knew a lot about me from Clay, but I don't know much about you," she said once the waitress had left. "Where are you from? Do you have other family?"

"My family lives in Oregon and it's a big one. I have three brothers and two sisters."

"Wow, that *is* big. Are you close?"

Quinn reached for a chip. "We're very close. A day doesn't go by that I don't get a phone call from a brother or sister or one of my parents. All my siblings are married with families of their own and they hate the idea that for the last five years I've been alone." He dipped the chip into the salsa, then popped it into his mouth.

"So how did you end up in Esperanza?"

"I went to school in San Antonio and fell in love with Texas. When I graduated, I started looking around the area for a small town that needed a veterinarian. Esperanza fit the bill. The vet at the time, Dr. Eliot Patterson, was about to retire and he invited me out here for a visit. I fell in love with the town and the people. What about you? Are your parents still alive?"

"The story of my parents is a twisted, sordid tale." She paused to take a sip of her drink, her eyes darkening. "My father was a used-car salesman named Ellis Mayfair who came through town twice a month to see my mother. At that time my mother was living in Sacramento. The short story is she got pregnant and Ellis wasn't happy about it. I was delivered by Ellis in a motel room. When my mother fell asleep Ellis gave me to a doctor who adopted me out in an illegal adoption. When my mother woke up and found out what he'd done, she stabbed him. He died and she went to prison."

"My God, Jewel." As he thought of his own family closeness, he wanted to grab her to him and hold her until he figured out a way to somehow change her history. As if losing her fiancé weren't enough, this bit of information made him realize just what kind of a survivor Jewel Mayfair really was.

"It's all right," she said hurriedly. "The story has a happy ending. Charlie and Ruth Baylor adopted me and raised me in a small town in Ohio. They couldn't have kids of their own and were loving, wonderful parents."

Although her smile was genuine as she spoke of her adoptive parents, the darkness that had deepened her eyes when she'd first spoken of her real mother and father didn't lift.

Quinn had a feeling there was more to the story than the thumbnail sketch she'd given him, but he was reluctant to pry too deep too fast. Still, he couldn't stop himself from probing a little more.

"Did you ever get a chance to know your real mother? Is she still in prison?"

Her fingers tightened around the stem of her glass. "No, she eventually got out of prison, and we managed to meet, but she passed away soon after that."

"I'm sorry." Once again he wanted to wrap his arms around her and hold her until the haunted darkness in her eyes receded. Instead, he decided a change of topic might be more appropriate. "So, how did you get involved with the Hopechest Ranch?"

Some of the tension left her face as she took another sip of her drink, then relaxed into the back of the chair. "Originally, I had my own small practice. Then when the accident happened, I pretty much fell apart. I gave up the practice and sort of drifted in a deep depression. It was my Aunt Meredith who suggested I spend a couple hours a week at the Hopechest Ranch in Prosperino, and when she decided to open the ranch here, she offered me this position and I jumped at the opportunity."

"It must be amazingly rewarding working with the children."

"It is, but I'm sure you feel the same way about your work with animals."

He nodded. "It's very rewarding and at times heartbreaking."

She smiled. "That defines my work at the ranch perfectly."

For a moment they were silent, but it was a comfortable silence. It lasted only a short time, then they began to speculate on Joe Colton's run to become president and talked about how excited Jewel was about Joe and Meredith's upcoming visit to Texas and the Hopechest Ranch. At some point during their conversation he noticed the stress that had lined her face easing and the shadows in her eyes backing away.

Quinn glanced at his watch, then back at her. "Look, it's almost six. I don't know about you, but smelling all the food cooking suddenly has me starving. How about we move to the other side and get some dinner."

"I'd like that," she said. Her immediate acquiescence both surprised and pleased him. He wanted to know more about her. He wanted to know everything about her and it had been a long time since he'd felt that way about a woman.

For the last five years Quinn had grieved deeply for the wife he'd lost, but now he was more than ready to share his life with a special woman. From the moment he'd seen Jewel, he'd had a feeling she might just be that woman and everything he'd learned about her and in the kiss they'd shared only made him more certain.

But there was no question that Jewel had secrets. He saw them in the dark places in her eyes and her quick movements to hide whatever it was she'd been doing in the library only emphasized that.

Quinn was a patient man and he was determined to unlock all the secrets that Jewel Mayfair possessed.

It's just dinner, that's what Jewel told herself. They were simply two adults enjoying the pleasure of each other's company over a meal.

Still, she couldn't deny that being in Quinn's company relaxed her, that the quiet steadiness of his nature drew her and calmed the chaotic noise inside her head.

Even with the rich scent of the Mexican food in the air, she could smell the scent of his cologne, a masculine woodsy scent that she found wonderfully appealing.

It was impossible for her not to think about the kiss they'd shared the night before. Just looking at his mouth made hers heat with the memory.

"Another margarita?" he asked as the waitress arrived to take their orders.

"No, thanks. One is definitely my limit." Instead they both ordered soft drinks to go along with their meals.

"I haven't had enchiladas for a long time." She placed her napkin in her lap.

"Mexican food is one of my favorites," he replied. "Along with Italian and Chinese and good old-fashioned American cuisine."

She laughed. "You sound like a man who just likes to eat."

"Guilty as charged." He reached up and pushed back a strand of his magnificent hair.

She smiled. "I've been thinking about getting some animals for the ranch, petting-zoo kinds of animals. Caring for them would be terrific therapy," she said.

"That's a wonderful idea," he agreed. "Unconditional love is what you get with animals. They don't care where you've been or what you've done. When you decide to do that, let me know and I'd be glad to go with you to purchase the animals you want."

"I'd appreciate it. I was thinking maybe some baby lambs and goats to start." No question, she was physically attracted to Quinn. There was a simmering sexuality about him that was even more appealing because he seemed so oblivious to it.

By the time the waitress arrived with their meals, he was entertaining her with stories about the various animals he'd encountered over the years.

She couldn't remember the last time she'd laughed as much and she'd forgotten how wonderful it was to share laughter with a good-looking man.

"Cocoa is the first animal I've ever owned," she confessed.

He looked at her in mock horror. "No dog when you were growing up? No pet rabbit or kitty or turtle?"

She shook her head. "Nothing. Ruth was allergic to pets and when I finally got out on my own, it just didn't seem that important."

"I've had a dog all my life. Right now I have a schnauzer. Sabra has been the only woman in my life for the last four years, but I'm hoping that's going to change."

There it was, that whisper of heat flashing in his eyes, a heat that said he liked what he saw when he looked at her. A responding warmth swept through her. Was she ready for a new relationship? The possibility shot a little thrill through her.

"Is Sabra the jealous type?" she asked in an attempt to keep things light.

"Not that I know of, although I've never had another woman in my house."

His words surprised her. "I would think all the single women in Esperanza would be banging down your door."

He grinned. "I have to admit, I have had a few questionable casseroles brought to my doorstep by some of the local women, but I just wasn't interested until lately in pursuing anything."

She had the distinct impression he was courting her.

He leaned forward. "I know I'm not the most exciting man on the block. I'm forty-four years old. I know my limits when it comes to drinking. I take my friendships very seriously and, except for last night, I usually don't kiss on the first date."

He was definitely courting her, and it was working. He didn't seem to have a clue that the picture he painted of himself was far more appealing than a wild bad boy. Solid and dependable—that's what Jewel wanted in a man.

As the waitress came to remove their plates and ask them about dessert, she declined, but Quinn insisted she needed some coffee and sopaipillas to complete the meal.

Laughing, she settled back to enjoy dessert with him. Her research into Andrew's death had long ago left her mind and being in Quinn's company made her feel as if somehow everything in her life was going to be all right.

They took turns dipping the puffed pastry into a bowl of honey and split the vanilla-bean ice cream that Quinn had added to the dessert order.

The conversation remained light and easy. They talked about their favorite foods, movies they liked and didn't like and mutual acquaintances they knew.

It was after eight when they finally left the restaurant and walked back to where their vehicles were parked at the library.

He walked her to her car and she leaned against the side and smiled up at him. "Thank you for dinner, Quinn. It was an unexpected pleasure."

He stepped closer to her, invading her personal space, but she didn't mind. Remembering how she'd felt the night before when his big strong arms had surrounded her, when his mouth had plied hers with heat, she definitely didn't mind at all that she sensed he wanted to kiss her again.

"I'd like to do it again," he said.

For a moment she thought he was talking about kissing her, then she realized he was talking about having dinner together.

"I'd like that," she replied. She found something almost hypnotically peaceful about being in his company, but it was a peacefulness coupled with a huge dose of an emotion that felt strongly like desire. And it had been so long since a man had moved her on any level.

"There's something else I'd like to do again." He took another step closer to her and this time there was no mistaking what he was talking about.

Her heart two-stepped as he reached out his hand

and with his index finger traced the outline of her lips. "Do you mind?" he murmured.

"No." The single word whispered out of her with a sigh of anticipation.

He leaned forward and took her mouth with his. He tasted of honey and coffee and a passion that was contagious.

Before things could spiral out of control, she ended the kiss. "Dr. Logan. I think you could be a dangerous man."

He stepped back from her and smiled. "If we were someplace more private, I'd like to be a lot more dangerous." His smile fell away and he gazed at her intently. "I like you, Jewel. You're the first woman since my wife whom I've wanted to spend time with and get to know better." He shifted from one foot to the other, as if uncomfortable as he waited for her to reply.

"And I'd like to get to know you better, too," she replied. "I'll tell you what. Sunday I'm planning on taking the kids on a trail ride at Clay's. With school starting Monday, I thought it would be a nice way to end the summer vacation. Why don't you plan on joining us?"

There was no better way to judge a man's true character than to see him interacting with children, she thought.

"I'd love to share a trail ride with you and the kids," he said without hesitation. "In fact, why don't you let me bring a picnic lunch for everyone?"

She laughed. "Are you out of your mind? I mean, I do have seven kids in residence at the moment."

"Then it's lunch for nine. Just tell me what time and I'll take care of the rest of the details."

"Okay," she said, helpless to turn down what appeared to be a heartfelt offer. "Why don't we plan on meeting at Clay's at eleven? We can ride for two hours then have lunch around one." As he nodded his agreement she opened her car door and slid in behind the wheel. "Good night, Quinn."

As she pulled out of the library parking lot and onto Main she couldn't stop herself from taking a quick glance in her rearview mirror to get one last look at him.

He stood by his truck watching her drive away and once again her heart fluttered with a sense of anticipation, of sweet possibility.

She turned on her headlights against the approaching darkness of night and wondered if it was possible that she was finally ready to look ahead instead of dwelling on a past she couldn't change.

Had her grief over Andrew and the baby ebbed to where she could entertain the idea of a new man in her life? She tightened her hands on the steering wheel. Maybe, she thought. Maybe it was the right time.

She liked Quinn and the more time she spent with him the more she liked him. He stirred up a desire inside her that half stole her breath away.

She glanced at her watch as she turned into the lane that led to the ranch. Good, she'd be just in time to tell the children good-night.

Funny, how the exhaustion that had weighed so heavily on her as she'd gone through the morning, the same exhaustion that had burned her eyes and ached in her shoulders at the library had disappeared while she'd been in Quinn's company.

He excited her and energized her while at the same time bringing to her a kind of inner peace she hadn't felt for a very long time. It was a heady combination.

Cheryl was in the kitchen when she got home. Jewel made the nighttime rounds to say good-night to the children, then she sat at the table and listened as Cheryl filled her in on the day.

"Mark had the kids do some acrylic oil painting today. He brought birdhouses for each of them to paint. The kids loved it and we now have seven interesting-looking bird houses to hang in the trees," Cheryl said.

"We'll have to see about getting them up this weekend. Maybe we can hang them in the trees out there so they can be admired while we have our meals." She pointed to the kitchen window.

"That would be nice," Cheryl agreed. "Barry had a bit of a meltdown this afternoon. His mother called and started talking about all the things that would be different when he got home. He got anxious, had a panic attack, then got angry. Jeff took him for a walk so he could cool down."

Jewel made a mental note to have a session with Barry first thing in the morning. She and Cheryl talked for a few more minutes, then they said their good-nights and parted ways.

Jewel went first into her sitting room, which served as her office and took a few minutes to make notes in Barry's file. Calls from his mother always upset him. Barry's father had died a year ago and within a month his mother had remarried. Almost immediately Barry had started having panic attacks with bursts of extreme rage. His mother seemed to be clueless that she hadn't given her son time to grieve the loss of his father.

She closed the file and yawned, her thoughts immediately shifting back to Quinn. She wondered how he had gotten the scar on his cheek. It actually enhanced his attractiveness, giving his face interesting character.

She was curious to see how he'd be with the kids. It was easy to enjoy the company of children who were well-behaved, but the children at the Hopechest Ranch were here because their behavior wasn't perfect.

Yawning again, she went into her master bath and got ready for bed. Maybe she'd read for a while. It was just after nine and she was in the middle of a new book by a famous psychologist detailing her work with borderline personality disorder.

Minutes later, snuggled in her bed with the bedside lamp on and her book in her arms, she tried to focus on the words, but her mind kept drifting back to the time she'd spent with Quinn.

There had been a time following Andrew's death and the loss of her baby that Jewel hadn't wanted to live, when the depression had been too huge for her to stand. The incapacitating grief had passed, but it wasn't until Quinn had gazed at her with his simmering topaz eyes that she felt as if she were truly alive again.

Even now, just thinking about him, her heart quickened and a smile curved her lips. She closed her book and placed it on the nightstand. Maybe if she went to sleep right away Quinn would fill her dreams. That would be so nice.

She shut off the light and burrowed back down beneath the crisp sheets. "No bad dreams tonight," she whispered in the dark. "Please, no bad dreams."

She closed her eyes and listened to the ordinary sounds of the house at rest, the soft hum of the air conditioner, the faint tinkle of the wind chimes that hung outside on the back patio. Familiar sounds, comforting noise that lulled her into that twilight state between consciousness and unconsciousness.

That's when she heard it—the sound of a baby crying—and even though she knew it was impossible, she knew it was *her* baby crying. She felt the mournful cries in the depth of her womb, in the center of her soul.

No, not again. Not tonight. The cries seemed to come from all around her and pierced through her with the sharpness of a needle.

"It's not real," she said aloud. But it sounded so real she wanted to leap out of bed and go searching for the baby she'd lost, the baby who cried for her from the beyond.

This had happened before. She'd heard this sound

before and had jumped out of bed and tried to find the source. She'd wandered the woods in search of the baby who needed her, who cried for her, and had found nothing.

She refused to leave her bed tonight. Instead, she clapped her hands over her ears as deep, wrenching sobs escaped her.

She knew the cries weren't real and yet they echoed through her with an authenticity that was heart-wrenching.

"Go away," she whispered. "Please, stop crying."

It seemed to last forever, but as suddenly as it had begun, it stopped.

Tears ripped from the very depths of her and she realized they weren't just tears for the baby she'd lost, but also because she realized now that she could never have anything with Quinn Logan. She could never have a relationship with any man.

There could only be one explanation for the baby's cries that haunted her, for the sound of Andrew's voice calling to her from the woods.

She was losing her mind.

Her mother had died in a mental institution, the lines between reality and madness so blurred and undefined that in the end she hadn't even known her own name.

As sobs racked through Jewel, she feared that was her future, that eventually the lines would blur for her and she'd wind up like her mother, alone with only her mental illness and locked away from the world.

# Chapter 6

Jewel had just finished the early morning watering of the flowers when an unfamiliar truck pulled up to the front of the house. The truck might be unfamiliar, but the man who climbed out of the driver's seat wasn't.

"Ryder!" She greeted him with a surprised smile.

"Hi, Jewel." His long legs carried him to where she stood. "Hope it's not too early for a visit."

"Of course not. Mornings start early here at the ranch. You want to come in for a cup of coffee? Some of Cheryl's blueberry muffins are probably left over from breakfast."

"No, thanks, I just finished breakfast." He raked a hand through his shiny black hair. "Actually, I'd like to talk to you about a job. You probably heard that

Ana is going to be teaching at the bilingual school. She starts in two weeks."

"No, I hadn't heard, but good for her. I know that's what she's always wanted to do. She'll make a wonderful teacher."

He nodded. "And I've decided to go back to school." His ebony eyes glittered with a newfound pride. "I want to be the best husband for Ana, the best father for Maria that I can be, and I've decided an education is the first step."

Jewel placed a hand on his forearm. "Good for you, Ryder. I'm sure Clay is proud of your decision."

"He is, but more important, I am. I'm committed to turning things around for myself. I'm here for a couple of reasons. I was wondering if you could use some part-time help and if there's a possibility that while I'm in school you'd be available to add Maria to your group of kids. To be honest, Ana and I wouldn't trust her in anyone else's care."

Jewel thought of the sweet baby girl and her heart expanded. "I think we could definitely work something out," she replied. "I've been thinking of having a pen built for some goats and lambs and small animals. Think you could handle that?"

He grinned. "Not a problem. I won't be starting school until the spring semester so until then I was hoping you could use me twenty to twenty-five hours a week."

She nodded and for the next few minutes they worked out the details of his employment and baby

Maria's care. She showed him the area on the side of the house where she wanted the pen and assured him that Jeff would be available to help.

As he got back into his truck to leave she waved, wondering if it had been a simple case of maturity or finding the love of a good woman that had turned the bad boy into a good man.

After he left, Jewel went back inside to grab her car keys and the list of school supplies that needed to be bought. "I'm off," she told Cheryl who was in the kitchen. "Thank goodness I can get this shopping done today and not have to be in town tomorrow. I hate shopping on Saturdays."

"Jeff and I have a whole day of shopping planned for tomorrow. I told him I want to drive into San Antonio and get me a good pair of shoes. All you can find around here are cowboy boots and sneakers."

Jewel smiled. "Make him take you out to lunch at one of those fancy restaurants on the river walk."

"I plan to," Cheryl replied.

Minutes later Jewel was in her car, headed toward Main Street. Since the moment she'd gotten out of bed that morning, she'd thought about calling Quinn to cancel the plans for Sunday.

After the horrible trauma of the night before, she didn't feel it was fair to give him false hope, to allow him to think that they could ever have a real relationship.

He'd made it more than clear that he was interested in her and, under different circumstances, she would have reciprocated. She liked the solidness of him, the gentle nature that she sensed he possessed. And if she were truthful with herself, she'd admit that she also loved the width of his shoulders, the simmer of sensuality that lit his eyes.

But how could she, in good conscience, follow her heart when she suffered visions of a dead man, heard the sounds of her baby crying out from the grave?

It would be best to call him and cancel, to stop whatever might happen between them now before one of them got hurt. The problem was she wasn't sure how to gracefully withdraw the invitation she'd extended. She could cancel the trail ride altogether, but that wasn't fair to the kids.

She sighed as she pulled into a parking space in front of the local discount store. It took her over an hour to get everything for the kids to start school Monday morning.

She was juggling her bags to the car when she saw Quinn walking toward her. Despite her desire to the contrary, her heartbeat raced a little faster at the sight of him.

"Let me help you with those," he said as he took two of the bags from her.

"School supplies," she said. "It's amazing what's required by the teachers these days."

He opened the back car door and put the bags he'd carried inside, then took the other two from her and stowed them, as well. When he turned to look at her, his eyes glowed with a warm light. "I just came from Miss Sue's café where I arranged for lunch for nine to be ready for Sunday. She's working on a real picnic menu—fried chicken and coleslaw and buttermilk biscuits."

"You shouldn't have done that," she protested in dismay. There was no way she could uninvite him knowing the trouble he'd already gone to.

"I don't mind. In fact, I'm really looking forward to it and you know I've never met a kid who didn't like fried chicken." He checked his watch. "Unfortunately, I've got to run. I've got an appointment with a horse. I'm looking forward to Sunday, Jewel." He said her name as if it were a caress.

She nodded and watched as he hurried off. Okay, so much for canceling Sunday's plans. Deciding to stop into Miss Sue's for a cup of coffee and a cinnamon bun, Jewel headed down the street toward the café.

As she walked, she realized that a part of her hadn't wanted to cancel, but instead yearned to spend another day in Quinn's company.

The kids would be with them, there would be no opportunity for him to kiss her again, to touch her in any way. She'd give herself that time with him and after Sunday she'd make sure they had no time alone together again.

A sadness swept through her as she realized that she was making the choice to be alone, but what other choice did she have? She would embrace her work, spend her life helping and loving other people's children. It would be enough because it had to be enough, but that didn't mean it didn't hurt.

Quinn Logan had suffered tremendously in burying a wife. She wouldn't want to add to his heartache by getting close to him, allowing him to care for her and in the end having to tell her goodbye as mental illness overwhelmed her.

What she hoped was that the auditory hallucinations were just a manifestation of her grief. Right now they only seemed to affect her at night, just before she fell asleep. She hoped that eventually they would stop, but feared what the future might bring.

The cowbell tingled as she walked through the door of the café. Immediately she saw Olivia Halprin and Sheriff Jericho Yates at one of the tables. They waved her over and insisted that she join them.

Olivia had appeared in town a couple of months ago, suffering from amnesia, and it was Jericho who had taken in the injured young woman. Jericho had taken her to his log cabin in the woods and there love had blossomed.

It was discovered that Olivia had worked for Governor Allan Daniels, the man running against Joe Colton for the party nomination. Olivia had uncovered a trail of crooked deals and bribery, and when her memory had finally returned, Allan Daniels had tried to silence her…permanently. Jericho had managed to save her life and the two had been inseparable ever since.

"How are things at the ranch?" Jericho asked as Jewel sat at their table.

"Fine. And how about your place? I heard through the grapevine that Olivia had been doing some decorating at the log cabin."

Jericho gave a mock frown. "She's put in some fufu things that have destroyed the rustic character of the cabin."

Olivia laughed and gave him a playful punch in the arm. "Don't let him fool you. He loves the changes I've made."

Jericho reached out and covered her hand with his. "Actually, that's true. She's made it a home."

"So do you know yet if it's a girl or a boy?" Jewel gestured toward Olivia's tummy.

"The doctor thinks it's a girl," Olivia replied. She smiled at Jericho and then looked back at Jewel. "And if it is, the sheriff has already told me we'll get right to work on a boy."

"That's nice. I'm so happy for you both. And is there a wedding in the future?"

"Absolutely," Jericho replied. "In the very near future."

As Jewel ate her cinnamon bun and drank a cup of coffee, she visited with the couple. There was no question that the two were deeply in love, and while Jewel was happy that they'd found each other, she felt the bittersweet pang of her own loneliness.

It was just after noon when she pulled back into the ranch and reminded herself that she needed to have a session with Barry that afternoon. She smiled as she saw all the kids out in the yard with Cocoa.

Jeff sat on the porch, watching as the kids chased the dog and the dog chased the kids. Jeff approached as Jewel got out of the car.

"We figured a little exercise would be good for Cocoa," he said as he grabbed two of the bags from the backseat.

"I'm not sure who's getting more, the kids or the dog," Jewel replied with a laugh.

"I'll tell you one thing, that dog is smart, but I don't think he's going to make it as any kind of a watchdog. He likes everyone too much. Deputy Rawlings stopped by earlier and I thought Cocoa was going to lick him to death."

Jewel laughed. "That's okay. He's not meant to be a watchdog. Did Adam say why he stopped by?"

"I got the feeling it was just a social visit. I'll take these bags inside for you." He grabbed all the bags while Jewel walked out in the yard to join the kids and Cocoa.

As she played with the dog and the children's laughter filled the air, she reminded herself that this was what was important. She told herself that she didn't need what Jericho and Olivia had found together, she didn't need anything but this ragtag family of troubled kids and the love of her family to sustain her. Maybe if she repeated that mantra enough times, she would actually believe it.

\* \* \*

Quinn arrived at Clay's place early on Sunday. It should have worried him, how anxious he'd been for this day to arrive. But instead he embraced his anticipation, for the first time in years feeling ready to move on with his life, ready to fall in love and fulfill the dreams he hadn't been able to fulfill with Sarah.

And he wanted to do it with Jewel. She both excited and intrigued him. When he was around her, he felt the expectation of something special about to happen, saw a glimpse into a future he desperately wanted to grab.

The food he'd picked up from Miss Sue's was packed in two large coolers and he arranged with Carlos, one of Clay's hands, to have it delivered to a specific place in the pasture around one o'clock.

He was in the stables, saddling up Noches, his black stallion, when Clay walked in. "I heard through the grapevine that you and Jewel were seen looking quite cozy at a certain Mexican restaurant the other day."

Quinn grinned. "Normally I'd tell you that you know better than to listen to the grapevine, but in this particular case, it's true."

"You'll never find a better woman than Jewel," Clay said. "She's had some tough breaks in her life. She deserves some happiness." There was an edge to Clay's voice, as if he was warning Quinn not to toy with Jewel.

Quinn clapped his friend on the back. "Down boy,

you know me better than to think I'd ever intentionally do anything to hurt her."

"I know. I just worry about her." Clay stepped back and leaned against the stable door. "But it sounds like you have a fun day planned for today."

"It should be fun." Quinn finished cinching the saddle and gave Noches a pat on his rump.

"And you talked to Carlos about the lunch details?"

"Yeah, thanks for letting him help out." Their conversation was interrupted by the sound of the minibus from the Hopechest Ranch pulling up.

Quinn stepped out of the stable and got a blood rush as he saw Jewel. She looked beautiful with her tousled golden-brown hair shining in the sun. Her brown eyes sparkled and her features were relaxed in a way he hadn't seen before. Worn, tight jeans fit her long legs to perfection and her pink T-shirt deepened the chocolate hue of her eyes.

In the first fifteen minutes Quinn tried to put faces with names as she introduced him to all the kids. Then it took another half an hour to get everyone on his or her horse and out of the stables.

They followed a well-worn horse trail across the pasture. The kids were in the lead and Quinn and Jewel brought up the rear, their horses side by side.

"You look great today," he said.

"Thanks, I feel pretty great. I've been looking forward to today, kind of a final celebration with the kids before school starts tomorrow."

He hoped she'd also been looking forward to

spending more time with him, but he didn't ask, was afraid of sounding too forward. He had a feeling he needed to take things slowly with her, that she was like a wounded animal that needed to be gentled. And that was one of Quinn's specialties.

It was impossible to have a real conversation with her during the ride. The kids yelled back and forth to one another and the horses whinnied and nickered as the sound of their hooves on the hard earth filled the air.

Still, Quinn always enjoyed riding Noches, who had just enough spirit to be challenging yet not enough to be unmanageable. And there was the additional benefit of being able to look sideways and see Jewel on the horse next to him.

She was a good rider and looked at ease in the saddle. She flashed him a bright smile and urged her horse into a trot, quickly moving to the front of the pack.

Quinn nudged Noches faster to catch up with her. Noches tossed his head, wanting to run like the wind, but Quinn held tight to the reins, refusing to give the stallion his head.

The trails led through the woods, across a small dry creek bed and then into open pasture. It was only then that Quinn allowed Noches to run. He flew ahead of the group with the wind in his face. The horse responded to his most subtle command. Quinn pulled in as he reached the far edge of the pasture and waited for the group to catch up with him.

"Pretty fancy riding, Dr. Logan," Jewel said.

"Maybe I'm showing off in an attempt to impress you," he replied.

She laughed. "Consider me impressed."

"Me, too," Carrie said as she rode up next to them. "Someday I want to ride that fast, but this dumb old horse won't do anything but walk."

Jewel smiled. "When you've had a little more experience on a horse, maybe we'll find you one that runs."

The ride continued until they came to a stand of trees where Carlos sat on a tractor with a small cart behind it containing the lunch coolers. Carlos unfastened the cart and with the promise to return for it later, he drove away.

They let the horses go to graze and Quinn pulled several large tablecloths from the first cooler and spread them on the ground.

Lunch was chaos and laughter. The kids talked almost as much as they ate and it was obvious they all adored Jewel. Jewel remained relaxed. She laughed often and the sound was music to Quinn's ears.

After lunch Quinn pulled several Frisbees from the cooler and led the kids in a game of catch. Jewel remained on the tablecloth and played cheerleader.

As the kids continued to toss the Frisbees back and forth, Quinn walked over and collapsed next to Jewel. "You're the cutest Frisbee cheerleader I've seen in a long time," he said.

"Have you seen a lot of Frisbee cheerleaders in your life?" she asked teasingly.

"Hundreds. Maybe thousands," he replied. "I travel the countryside seeking Frisbee cheerleaders."

"We both know you're full of beans, as the kids would say."

He laughed and looked over where the kids were playing catch. "They're a nice bunch," he observed.

She smiled. "They know you are responsible for giving us Cocoa so they're on their best behavior with you. Trust me, they aren't always this easy to get along with."

"Kelsey doesn't seem to be having as much fun as the others."

Jewel frowned as her gaze went to the dark-haired girl who stood slightly separated from the others, hands shoved in her pockets.

"Kelsey has spent the last couple of years being shuttled from relative to relative. She's terrified to embrace any kind of happiness because she's afraid it will be taken away from her."

"That's the way I felt right after Sarah died."

Jewel turned to look at him, her gaze curious. "You're so much more open than I thought you'd be. Clay had told me you were the strong, silent type."

He smiled. "Normally I *am* pretty quiet, but I've been working on changing that." He looked back at the kids and frowned thoughtfully. "After Sarah died I realized there were so many things I hadn't said to her, so many thoughts I hadn't shared. I decided I'd never let that be a regret again."

Their discussion was interrupted as Lindy joined

them on the blanket, her face flushed from her exertions. "I've gotta rest," she exclaimed. "I'm pooped, but I think maybe another piece of chicken would give me my energy back."

Quinn grinned at her. "There's only one thing better than a piece of fried chicken." He reached into the cooler and pulled out a container of chocolate cupcakes.

Lindy's eyes lit up and she turned to where the other kids were still playing with the Frisbees. "Hey, guys, we got cupcakes," she yelled, sparking a stampede as they all ran for dessert.

It was almost five by the time they made their way back to the stables. "They'll all sleep well tonight," Jewel said as she brushed down her horse.

"Nothing like fresh air and sunshine to bring on a good night's sleep," Quinn replied. He didn't want the day to end. While he'd enjoyed his interaction with the kids, he didn't feel as if he'd had enough time with Jewel.

He led Noches into his stall, then returned to where Jewel was finishing up with her horse. "I have an idea. Why don't you take the kids home and get them settled in then meet me back here for a sunset ride."

She looked up at him and in her eyes he saw indecision. "Come on, Jewel," he urged. "There's nothing more beautiful that a horseback ride at sunset. Meet me back here about seven-thirty." He smiled at her. "I promise you it will be a painless experience."

She smiled then and nodded. "Okay, you talked me into it."

"Great, then I'll meet you back here."

A few minutes later Jewel went with the kids and Quinn left to go home to check on the animals either boarding with him or recovering from illnesses.

Quinn lived in a three-bedroom ranch house. It was simple and efficient but he spent most of his time in the front building, which was the heart of his veterinary practice. The building was divided into four areas—a small office, an area for boarding animals, an examination room and an operating room.

He checked on the boarders, made sure they had food and water, then decided to shower the day's dirt off before the ride with Jewel.

As he redressed in a clean pair of jeans and a navy T-shirt, he tried not to think about what he'd really like to do with Jewel. He'd love to take her on their sunset ride, then dismount and make love to her beneath a starry sky.

She'd confused him today. There had been a distance in her eyes. She'd been more closed off than before, as if afraid to share too much of herself with him.

He didn't want to screw up by pushing her too fast and yet a part of him thought she needed a nudge back into life. He was so ready to embrace her, to embrace love again but, more than anything, he wanted to discover the source of the darkness he sometimes saw in her eyes, a darkness that worried and confused him.

# Chapter 7

Jewel hadn't intended to agree to the sunset ride. She knew Quinn liked her, but it wasn't fair to make him think that there was any chance for a romance between them.

But she felt such deep loneliness and so enjoyed his company. It was difficult to deny herself the pleasure of spending more time with him. Maybe they could become good friends.

She stood beneath a hot stream of water in her shower and tried to imagine just being friends with Quinn. It would never work. Friends didn't want to kiss friends and now that she knew what Quinn tasted like, how she felt in his arms, she would never be satisfied with just a simple friendship. And she had a feeling he wouldn't be, either.

"You're overthinking," she said aloud as she stepped out of the shower. That was the problem with being a psychologist, sometimes she analyzed way too much.

She put on a clean pair of jeans and a short-sleeved cotton blouse. Even when the sun went down, it was still warm, despite being the beginning of September.

She was just ready to walk out the door when Adam Rawlings pulled up. As usual, not one of his dark brown hairs was out of place as he got out of his car and ambled toward the porch.

She stepped outside to greet him. "Evening, Adam."

"Jewel." His brown eyes gazed at her intently. "Haven't seen you around lately."

"I've been busy, you know with school starting tomorrow and all."

"You need to take some time off." He smiled, his brown eyes warm and inviting. "Maybe see a movie with me or go out for a nice meal."

"I appreciate the thought, Adam, but now just isn't a good time for me. Maybe when things calm down around here." This wasn't the first time he'd asked her out and he never seemed offended that she never agreed to go out with him.

Perhaps she should. He'd certainly be a safe date for her because she felt absolutely no sparks with him. Unlike Quinn, who by merely looking at her could set her very skin on fire.

"You need to focus on yourself, Jewel," he said,

concern radiating from his eyes. "It's a great thing what you do here for these kids, but you should remember that you're a young woman who should have a life of her own."

"Thanks, Adam. Actually, I was just on my way out." She couldn't very well tell him she was on her way to meet another man, so she offered no other explanation.

"Then at least let me walk you to your car," he replied.

She nodded and stepped off the porch. "Everyone has been talking about the Coltons coming to town," he said as they walked to the garage. "It's not every day we get the man who's probably going to be president, and his wife in Esperanza."

"I can't wait," she exclaimed. The thought of seeing Meredith and Joe again filled her with warmth. "I'm planning a good old-fashioned Texas barbecue here during their visit."

"Sounds like a good time. I'm sure you'll want Jericho and all of us deputies here for additional security."

"I want you here as guests, as well," she replied. She punched the button on her remote to raise her garage door. "It will be a wonderful day filled with family and friends."

"Those are the best kind of days," he agreed. "I'll just say good night now and let you get on your way."

"Thanks, Adam."

He cocked an eyebrow upward. "For what?"

"For always checking in with me…for caring."

He smiled and there was a fierce intensity in his gaze. "I do care." He nodded a goodbye, then turned on his heels and went back to his car.

Jewel got into her car and backed out of the garage as Adam disappeared into his. He was a nice man. He had a great body for a man who was forty years old. Funny, she'd never heard him talk about any family. She assumed he was no stranger to loneliness, either.

The minute she pulled out of her driveway, thoughts of Adam disappeared as Quinn filled her mind. The sun hung low in the sky. Another thirty minutes and it would be sunset.

When she pulled up in front of Clay's stable, Quinn was already there, both his horse and the one she'd ridden that afternoon saddled and ready to go.

She couldn't help the way her heart leapt at the sight of him, so tall, so strong-looking and with that smile that made her feel as if she were the most important person in his world.

As she got out of the car and approached him, she couldn't help the lightness that filled her heart, the emotion that felt remarkably like joy.

"Hi," he said.

"Hi, yourself. Looks like you've got us all ready to go."

"I've even got a bottle of wine and a couple of glasses tucked into my saddlebag for a sunset toast."

"Wine and a sunset—sounds like the perfect ending

to a day," she said. And of course, there was also the handsome hunk to add to the heady combination.

She was glad she'd come. As they mounted the horses, she told herself not to think, not to analyze, but rather just to enjoy the beauty of the night and Quinn's company.

At a leisurely pace, they followed the same trails that they'd ridden earlier in the day. For a few minutes, neither of them spoke. It was a peaceful silence, one that didn't demand to be broken.

Birds flitted from tree to tree, emitting their last melodic songs of the day and a faint breeze provided a pleasurable relief from the afternoon's heat.

"I enjoyed the kids this afternoon," he said, finally breaking the silence.

"They think you're awesome," Jewel replied. She'd been impressed watching him interact with the kids. He'd treated each of them with respect and kindness. He'd listened patiently to all of them and she'd known instinctively that it hadn't been just an act for her benefit.

"Kelsey seemed a bit standoffish."

Jewel nodded. "She's afraid to be happy. I'm trying to teach her that happiness isn't a constant state of being and you need to grasp it when it comes and hold tight."

He frowned. "It's a shame a child that young has to have that kind of fear."

"You like kids." It was a comment rather than a question.

He nodded. "I do. I always wanted a big family

of my own. Unfortunately, it just wasn't in the cards for me."

"You still have time," she protested. "It's not as if you're over the hill."

He grinned and reached up to sweep his hair away from his eyes. "No, but sometimes I feel like I'm halfway up that hill."

She laughed. "If you're halfway up the hill, then I'm right behind you."

For the next few minutes they kept a slow pace and talked about the afternoon and each of the children. "Carrie told me she loved Cocoa but she really, really loved kittens," he said. "And Barry told me he'd love to have a lizard." He flashed her a grin. "I think I may have started something."

Jewel laughed again. "Maybe I can satisfy them with the goats and sheep I intend to get once I have a nice pen ready. I hired Ryder to work on building the pen."

"What's the story on Ryder and Clay's father? I've always gotten the feeling that things weren't great between them all."

"Ryder, Clay and Georgie are Uncle Graham's children from an affair he had while he was unhappily married to Cynthia, who was an extremely wealthy woman. Although everyone said he truly loved their mother, Mary Lynn Grady, he loved money more and so refused to leave his wife."

"It's a foolish man who would choose money over love."

"Uncle Graham has been on the outs with the family for a long time," she continued. "I think Uncle Joe tried to be close to him and gave him one opportunity after another to do right, but Uncle Graham continued to make bad choices and I think it hurts Uncle Joe that the two don't have any kind of a relationship now." She smiled ruefully. "Aren't you sorry you asked?"

"Not at all. To be honest, I find the Colton family history fascinating. It makes me realize how truly boring my family is."

"I'm sure the Coltons would have gladly taken a little more boring over the years," she replied.

They rode to the spot where they'd had lunch earlier in the day, then dismounted. Quinn pulled a blanket from his saddlebag, along with the wine and two glasses.

They sat side by side as the sun dipped lower in the sky, spreading out the last gasp of daylight in vivid pinks and oranges.

"To a beautiful sunset and a beautiful woman," Quinn said as he raised his wineglass to hers.

The toast might have sounded cheesy coming from any other man, but the light in his eyes told her the words came from his heart.

She stretched out on her side on the blanket and propped herself up on an elbow. "You should find a nice woman, Quinn."

He laid down facing her and crooked an eyebrow upward. "I have," he replied.

She shook her head. "You need somebody without baggage. Unfortunately, I have a ton."

"I don't know if you've noticed or not, but I have big, strong shoulders."

"Trust me, I've noticed," she replied dryly.

"Then why don't you trust me?" His eyes held her gaze intently.

She broke the eye contact and instead took a sip of her wine and stared at the sunset slowly fading into a night sky. "It's not that easy," she replied softly.

He reached out and covered one of her hands with his. "You can trust me, Jewel. You can tell me whatever is on your mind, anything, anytime."

She pulled her hand out from beneath his, finding his touch far too pleasurable. "You don't know anything about me. You have no idea where I come from."

"Then tell me. But hear me, Jewel. I can't imagine anything you'd tell me that would change my mind about you." His deep voice held a certainty that sent a rush of warmth through her.

"Did you know that my mother and Meredith Colton were twins?" she asked.

"No. I hadn't heard that," he replied. He showed no surprise at her seemingly abrupt change of topic.

"After my mother got out of prison for killing my father, she attacked Meredith. Meredith had amnesia and my mother switched identities with her. My mother impersonated Meredith for almost ten years while Meredith suffered amnesia and in those ten years my mother wreaked havoc on Joe's life."

"And what does this have to do with you, Jewel?" His tone was as gentle as the night breeze that caressed her skin. He moved closer to her, so close she could smell the scent of his cologne, feel the heat from his body radiating over her.

"Your mother was obviously a troubled woman, but I've seen you with your kids, I know the kind of heart you have, and if you thought by telling me about your mother I'd back off, then you were wrong." He set his wineglass aside.

This man was killing her with his heated eyes and his open heart. She wanted to tell him that she heard voices in the night, that phantom baby cries ripped at her guts. She wanted to warn him that she might be as unstable as her mother had been, but at that moment he reached out and touched her lips with his index finger.

"I want you, Jewel and the only thing that will make me back off is if you tell me that you don't want me." With a slow deliberation, he took her wineglass from her and set it just off the blanket.

She knew he intended to kiss her and even though she told herself she shouldn't let it happen, she shouldn't want it, want him so badly, she did.

He gathered her into his arms and kissed her. Soft and gentle, his lips whispered against hers and her heart fluttered in response.

Was it wrong of her to want him even knowing that she wouldn't, couldn't have a long-term relationship with him? If it was wrong at this moment, she didn't care. All she wanted was for him to hold her forever, for him to keep kissing her until she lost the capacity to think.

She opened her mouth, urging him to deepen the kiss. His tongue touched her bottom lip, then delved deeper to swirl with her own.

His hands moved up and down her back, caressing lightly as she tightened her arms around his neck. She leaned into him, wanting full contact with his lean, hard body.

Night shadows deepened and still they kissed, the only noise the sound of the horses shuffling their hooves nearby and Jewel and Quinn's quickened breathing.

She wanted more. The yearning that filled her was so intense that she could think of nothing but Quinn and her need to have him make love to her.

Her fingers found a button on his shirt and she unfastened it, wanting to run her hands over his bare chest. He released a small gasp as she unfastened another button, but his mouth didn't move from hers.

She used both hands, eager to get the shirt unbuttoned, and when she did, she slid her hands over his sculpted, hard chest. His skin was fevered heat and she loved the feel of his muscles, his bare flesh, beneath her fingertips.

He slid his hands up beneath her blouse, his palms warming her from the outside in, firing a desire in her to have more from him. His mouth lifted from hers but only to move to her cheek, then to the sensitive spot just behind her ear.

She was lost…lost in his touch, lost in the sensations that he evoked inside her. She wanted to stay in this pasture with him forever, with his mouth on hers, with his hands warming all the cold places in her heart and the night air surrounding them. But without warning he dropped his arms from around her and sat up.

He raked a hand through his thick mane of hair and released a deep sigh. "Not like this, Jewel," he said. "I want you so badly it hurts, but not like this. Not in a pasture. I want you in a soft bed with sheets to cuddle beneath and the entire night stretching out before us."

"Then take me home, to my bed and stay the night with me," she replied. She was shocked by her own words, but that didn't mean she wanted to take them back.

Just one night. She wanted just one night with him, with no sense of reason interfering, no common sense at play. She wanted one night of not thinking, of keeping the ghosts at bay.

He placed his palm on her cheek, the heat in his gaze igniting a faster burn inside her. "Are you sure that's what you want?"

"I've never been more sure of anything in my life," she replied.

In one fluid motion he stood and held out a hand to her. She reached for his hand and he pulled her to her feet and back into his arms. "I think I've wanted you since the very first time I laid eyes on you."

She looked up at him. "I feel the same way."

He released her and without saying another word he grabbed the wine bottle and glasses, then the blanket and stowed them back in his saddlebag.

As they rode back to the stable, she waited for a whisper of caution to flit through her head, a protest against what she was about to do, but all she felt was a calm peacefulness sweeping through her as she thought of spending the night in Quinn's arms.

Stars had begun to twinkle overhead, along with a half-sliced pie moon. The horses moved quickly toward home, as if they sensed their riders' eagerness.

When Jewel and Quinn reached the stables, it took only minutes for them to unsaddle the horses and get them into the appropriate stalls. Jewel then got into her car and headed for home with Quinn following in his truck.

She wouldn't be able to write this off as a crazy, impulsive move made in the heat of the moment. At any time during the ride back from the stables she could have changed her mind, but she didn't.

She wasn't giving him forever; she wasn't promising a thing. Consenting adults slept together all the time—it didn't have to mean anything except a single night of pleasure.

When she reached the ranch, she pulled into the garage, then stood by the door while Quinn parked and got out of his car.

He walked toward her and she felt the thrum of sexual excitement singing through her veins. She didn't remember feeling this intense hunger for Andrew. Making love with Andrew had been warm and fuzzy, not hot and edgy and that's exactly how Quinn made her feel.

When he reached where she stood by the front door, she felt his hesitation. "I'm only going to ask you this one last time," he said. "Are you sure about this? I've got to warn you, I'm not the kind of man who wants to make love to you then sneak out like a thief in the night."

She answered him by opening the front door and pulling him inside. The house was quiet and she led him through the entry and into her private quarters.

When she'd left the room hours earlier she'd had no idea that Quinn would be here with her, in her private, intimate space.

Although the room was quite large, he filled it with his presence. He held her gaze as he unbuttoned his shirt once again and shrugged it off his shoulders. His muscled chest gleamed in the light on her nightstand. He sat on the edge of the bed and took off his boots and socks, then stood once again.

Her throat went dry and her knees threatened to buckle as his hands moved to the button on his jeans. A rush of heat went through her, watching him step out of his jeans, leaving him only in a pair of low-riding navy briefs.

He came toward her with slow, deliberate movements, then unfastened the buttons on her blouse. When he was finished, he shoved the material off her shoulders and it fell to the floor behind her. His lips claimed hers once again and he cupped her breasts through the thin lace of her bra.

She unhooked her jeans, wanting nothing more than to be naked with him, to feel his hot, firm flesh against her own. He broke the kiss as she peeled off her jeans, then she walked over to the bed and slid in beneath the covers.

He grabbed his wallet from his jeans, set it on the nightstand, then joined her in the bed and wrapped her up in his arms as their lips met in a fiery kiss of desire.

The kiss continued while he unfastened her bra, swept the garment away as if it offended him, then captured her breasts in his hands. She hissed with pleasure as his thumbs raked over her taut nipples.

"You are so beautiful," he murmured, his mouth laving hers. He raised up just enough to stare down at her face. "You have no idea how much I want you."

"It can't be anymore than how much I want you," she replied.

He dipped his head and captured one of her nipples with his mouth. Sweet sensations of both pleasure and want crashed through her as she tangled her fingers in his thick, soft hair.

It didn't take long for them to rid themselves of the last of their underwear and their caresses grew even more intimate. She loved the smooth skin on his chest, broken only by a smattering of hair in the center. She loved the smell of him, a scent of the outdoors coupled with woodsy cologne and clean male.

He seemed to be in no hurry as he nibbled on her ear, slid his hot, hungry mouth down her throat, explored her inner thigh with his hands and moved her closer and closer to explosive peaks.

Refusing to be a passive partner, Jewel discovered that he moaned with pleasure when she ran her hand across his lower abdomen, close but not touching where she knew he wanted her to. He gasped as she licked his flat male nipples.

They caressed and tasted each other like two people who had been sensory-deprived for an eternity. His fingers finally found the very center of her, sliding against her moist heat, and she arched to meet him, need clawing at her, taking her up to new heights.

As she felt the approaching climax, she clung to him. Every muscle in her body stiffened and tremors of pleasure rocked through her, leaving her gasping and spent, yet wanting more.

She reached down and encircled the hard length of him, reveling in his moan of pleasure as she stroked him. He only allowed her touch for a moment, then he rolled her over on her back and reached for his wallet on the nightstand.

It took him only seconds to put on a condom, then move on top of her and between her thighs. For just a moment he remained poised above her, his eyes glowing like those of a wild animal.

In that moment, she felt more loved, more cherished then she ever had in her life. It was in the tenderness, in the hunger of his golden-brown eyes.

As he eased into her she closed her eyes, giving herself to the magic of his lovemaking. And it *was* magic. He entered her and paused to kiss her with a gentleness that stole her breath away.

He began to move against her, back and forth with slow, even strokes intended to produce the most pleasure. She raised her legs and locked them around his back, urging him deeper and faster as she felt the build once again begin.

Crying his name over and over again, she was lost in the act, in him. They moved faster, frenzied, and their pants and gasps filled the room.

She was there again, crashing down with earth-shattering tremors. He cried out her name as his own release washed over him. He shuddered once... twice, then remained still, his weight supported on his elbows as he sought to catch his breath.

He placed his hands on either side of her face and kissed her. "I'll be right back. Don't go away." He rolled out of the bed and padded into the adjoining bathroom.

Jewel felt weak with sated pleasure. She felt as if she had melted into the mattress and only an atomic bomb could force her to get up.

Quinn returned to the bedroom, and she turned off the bedside lamp. She was glad he wasn't dressing to leave but instead slid back into the bed and pulled her into his arms.

She lay with her upper body across his chest and she reached out a finger and touched the scar on his cheek. "How did you get that?"

He smiled. "Her name was Molly and she was the meanest mare I've ever met. I was working on her shoulder, where she had a sore, and she reared up and knocked me in the face then stomped on me."

She looked at him, horrified. "I had no idea being a veterinarian was so dangerous."

"I was young and careless and wasn't as wary as I should have been. It was as much my fault as it was hers."

"I'm glad you didn't jump back into your clothes and backpedal out of here." Jewel released a soft sigh and placed her head on his chest where the sound of his heartbeat was strong.

He stoked her hair with his big, strong hand. "As far as I'm concerned, the cuddle time afterward is almost as important as making love."

She sighed again, surprised to find her eyelids heavy with sleep. Her body fit perfectly against his and each caress of her hair brought sleep closer and closer.

"Quinn? Sometimes I have nightmares," she said, feeling as if she needed to warn him in case she had a bad night.

He slid his hand from her hair down her back, his palm like a miniature heating pad against her skin. "You won't tonight, Jewel."

He said the words with such confident assurance that she believed him. They shifted positions. She turned on her side and he spooned around her back, an arm flung over her as if in protection. Feeling more safe than she had in years, Jewel slept.

## Chapter 8

Jewel awakened to early morning sunlight filtering in through the curtains at her window. Her first thought was that there had been no dreams, no ghostly cries from the beyond. She had slept deeper and longer than she had since the death of Andrew and their unborn child.

Her second thought was of Quinn. She turned over in the bed and found herself alone. He must have crept out earlier and she was almost grateful. She would not have to explain to Jeff or Cheryl and the children why the handsome vet was in the house before breakfast.

Rolling over on her back to stare up at the ceiling fan, her head filled with visions of the night she'd shared with him. Just the memory caused her to tingle from head to toe.

He'd been a wonderful lover, both gentle and commanding and it frightened her more than a little how much she would love to repeat the experience.

But she couldn't. She'd already been unfair to him by allowing last night to happen. She knew Quinn wasn't the kind of man to take his relationships lightly and that would make everything more difficult.

She couldn't date Quinn knowing that she would never, could never fully commit to him. It wouldn't be fair to him and ultimately her.

Time to distance herself, she thought as she got out of bed and padded into the bathroom, then got into the shower. Even though she had slept dreamlessly last night in his arms, that didn't mean that she would no longer be haunted by Andrew and the baby she had lost.

It wouldn't bother her so much if she only heard Andrew softly calling her name and the baby crying in her dreams, but there had been far too many nights when she'd been wide-awake and had heard them.

And that's when the true haunting began, when she remembered her last visit with her mother in the mental ward. Patsy had been lost to the world, muttering incoherently and laughing inappropriately, hearing voices that weren't there, answering questions that nobody had asked.

As Jewel dressed she heard the sound of the children in the kitchen getting ready for breakfast. They were louder this morning, their voices filled with first day of school jitters.

Initially, Jewel had considered having her kids homeschooled, but ultimately she'd decided that interacting with the kids in town would be far healthier for them than isolation and the feeling that they were different. Besides, she wanted the town residents, who had harbored reservations about a ranch for troubled kids, to see that these kids weren't a threat.

An hour later she stood by the road that ran in front of the Hopechest Ranch, waiting for the school bus to appear. The sun overhead was brutal even at this time of the morning. The morning weather report had indicated that for the next week or two the temperatures were supposed to be well above normal.

"And the bus will bring us right back here after school, right?" Barry asked for the fourth time.

"The bus driver will drop all of you off at this very same spot," Jewel assured him.

"I hope my teacher likes me," Lindy exclaimed.

"Don't worry," Kelsey said, and placed a hand on Lindy's shoulder. "What's not to like?"

Jewel's heart warmed as she saw the older girl reassuring Lindy. It was the first sign she'd seen from Kelsey that she was reaching out, forming bonds, and that was important.

The bus lumbered into sight, spewing up a cloud of dust. It was only eight in the morning and already Jewel felt as if she could use another shower.

She saw the kids off, waving until the bus roared out

of sight, then she turned and walked back to the house. She'd just reached the porch when Ryder arrived.

Maria wasn't with him and he explained that Ana was home today with the baby. Her school wasn't to start until the following week.

"Gonna be a hot one today," she said.

"Supposed to be vicious for the next couple of weeks," he replied. "I've got the supplies coming for the pen this morning."

"Great, but make sure you stay hydrated while you're working out here," she cautioned. "Come inside and cool off whenever you need to."

He flashed her a grin. "Don't worry, I won't let the heat defeat me."

"I don't want to push you, but I'd love for the pen to be up and functioning by the time Meredith and Joe come to town."

"That's what, two weeks from now? I'm hoping Jeff and I will be able to have it knocked out by next weekend. That will give you a week to get the animals you want for the kids."

"Sounds perfect," Jewel replied.

With a wave he headed toward the area where the pen would be constructed. Jewel went back into the house.

"If it's okay with you, Jeff and I would like to take the kids on that field trip we talked about next Saturday or the Saturday after that," Cheryl said as the two women sat at the table and sipped a cup of coffee.

"The week after would work out perfect for me,"

Jewel replied thoughtfully. "While you're all gone, there are some things I want to do around here to prepare for the barbecue I'm planning for Joe and Meredith."

"Great! I'll tell Jeff we're on," Cheryl replied. The phone rang and she jumped up to answer it. She held out the phone to Jewel. "It's Quinn Logan for you." She covered the mouthpiece as Jewel hesitated.

"Tell him I'll call him back," she finally said. Her heart ached as Cheryl delivered the message. She'd love to hear his voice this morning, to tell him that she'd slept better in his arms last night than on any night since she'd arrived in Esperanza. But what was the point when she intended nothing more between them?

"Everything all right?" Cheryl asked, hanging up the phone.

"Fine, I just didn't feel like any social chitchat this morning. I'm going to go back to my office and catch up on some paperwork," she said, feeling the need to escape Cheryl's skeptical gaze.

Once she was at her desk, she leaned her head back against the chair and forced herself to think of anything but Quinn.

That day in the library—when she'd been researching the accident that had forever changed her life—seemed like months ago. She realized that she hadn't followed up on any of the information she'd learned that day.

What ever happened to James Corrs after Andrew

had turned him in for tax evasion? She hadn't gotten that far before Quinn had interrupted her.

With the kids at school and no fear of interruption she logged onto the Internet and searched for news articles related to James Corrs. It didn't take her long to find what she was searching for. James Corrs had gone to prison for federal tax evasion. He'd been sentenced to fifteen years. That was a long time to spend behind bars.

Before going to prison had he paid Andrew back by ramming into her car? What she wanted to do was call the authorities in California and have them reopen the case, investigate fully James Corrs as a suspect in the fatal hit-and-run.

But she knew what they would say. The accident had been ruled just that, they had other crimes to investigate and couldn't spend the time or manpower on a hit-and-run that had happened almost three years ago.

Wrapping her arms around her shoulders, plagued by a chill despite the warmth of the room, she thought about that moment when she'd awakened from one of her nightmares and had found the news clipping lying next to her.

It was crazy to think that somebody had snuck into the house and placed the clipping on her bed for her to find. But it was no more crazy than the logical explanation that she'd gotten up in her sleep and had dug the clipping out of a box of keepsakes.

Quinn had kept the ghosts at bay last night. It had been the first time in a very long time that she hadn't suffered any nightmares or heard voices or crying in the night.

Once again she found herself fighting the impulse to pick up the phone and return his call. Instead, she got up from her desk and decided to head over to Tamara and Clay's. They'd pulled a fast one eloping. Jewel wanted to hear all the details from Tamara and hadn't had an opportunity to talk to Tamara since learning the news.

Maybe part of the reason she wanted to talk to Tamara was because she knew her friend had never really warmed up to Quinn. By talking to her, Jewel could get the man out of her brain and would be able to forget the crazy yearning she had to fall back into his arms.

She drove the short distance to Clay's and parked in front of his house. She stepped out of the coolness of the car and the midmorning heat slapped her in the face.

Tamara answered her knock, her pretty face lighting with a smile. "Jewel, what a pleasure. Come on in."

"Thanks, I just thought I'd pop in for a quick visit. Is this a bad time?"

Tamara linked arms with her and walked her toward the kitchen. "Actually, it's a perfect time. I was just getting ready to have a glass of iced tea."

"Sounds wonderful. I can't believe how hot it is."

Tamara unlinked her arm with Jewel's and pointed her to the table. "And according to the weather reports it's only supposed to get worse. So I guess you're at loose ends today with the start of school."

Jewel smiled. "It's going to be strange having the kids gone during the weekdays."

"And I hear you have a new houseguest." Tamara set a glass of tea in front of Jewel then poured herself one and joined her at the table.

Jewel frowned. "A new houseguest?"

"Woof woof," Tamara replied.

Jewel laughed. "Ah, you mean, Cocoa. Yes, it was Quinn's idea." It was a perfect segue into the topic she most wanted to discuss. "I always got the impression you didn't much like Quinn."

Tamara smiled. "I have to confess that when he had to make the decision to put down Clay's stud, I hated the man. It was purely an emotional response. I saw how that decision hurt Clay and I guess it was kind of like killing the messenger. But since I've been back here I've changed my mind. Clay is constantly telling me what a stand-up guy Quinn is and I have to confess, I agree."

She raised an eyebrow. "Do I sense some interest there? Is it possible Adam Rawlings has some competition for your affections? Adam certainly hasn't hidden the fact that he has the hots for you."

"Unfortunately, the feeling isn't mutual and no, there's no interest with Quinn." The lie left a bad taste in her mouth. "I think I'm one of those women who are best alone."

"Human beings are not meant to be alone,"

Tamara countered. "We're built to thrive when loved and when loving. Trust me, Jewel, I tried it alone and it's not all it's cracked up to be. If you have an interest in the handsome vet, I say go for it."

For the next three days Jewel thought of Tamara's words. Quinn called several times each day and if Cheryl didn't answer and take a message, Jewel let the machine pick up.

She knew it was only a matter of time before she had to face him. What worried her was that she knew she was weak as far as he was concerned and for both of their sakes she had to stay strong. She had to stay away from him.

It had been four days since Quinn had heard from Jewel and he didn't intend to let another day pass without speaking with her.

It was obvious that she was avoiding his phone calls, so this morning he refused to give her a chance to escape him. At eight o'clock he parked his truck at the end of her driveway, where he assumed the school bus would pick up the kids.

He got out of the truck and walked around to the back, where he sat on the edge of the bed and waited. He wasn't sure what was up with her. When he'd left her bed in the predawn hours after making love with her, he'd believed that they were on their way to building something meaningful, something magic.

He couldn't accept that he'd simply imagined the

way she'd responded to him, not only in bed but also on their sunset ride when they'd shared pieces of themselves with each other.

Something had spooked her and he was determined to get to the bottom of it. She was the first woman who had captured his interest since his wife's death, and he wanted her to be the last.

The sun beat down on his shoulders as he watched the house. Maybe he'd rushed things with her. They'd gotten intimate so fast. Maybe he should have spent more time courting her. But there was no question that he felt an enormous passion for her, a passion that was hard to deny.

He sat up straighter as he saw the front door open and the kids began to spill out. Jewel followed them with Cocoa on a leash and he saw the exact moment she spied him. Her shoulders went rigid and she slowed her pace as if dreading what lay ahead. He was shocked by the quick stab of pain that coursed through him at her reaction.

Cocoa, on the other hand jumped and leapt with eagerness as soon as the dog saw him. "Dr. Quinn." Lindy greeted him with a wide smile. "Did you come to see us get on the bus?"

Sam tapped her on the back. "Duh, he's here to see Miss Jewel."

"I got here extra early so I could see all of you," Quinn replied.

"See, he wanted to see us get on the bus," Lindy exclaimed in triumph.

Quinn smiled at Jewel. "You've been a difficult lady to get in touch with the last couple of days." *Keep it light,* he told himself. He took a step toward her and petted Cocoa.

"Things have been crazy around here this week," she replied, her gaze not quite reaching his.

"Too crazy for a quick phone call?" A note of censure crept into his voice.

Before she could reply, the bus appeared. It wasn't until the kids were loaded and the bus pulled away that he spoke again. "Did I move too fast?"

She finally looked at him. "No, it's nothing you did wrong. It's me. I've just realized I'm not ready for any kind of a relationship."

"You seemed more than ready for one before we fell into bed with each other," he replied.

Her cheeks turned pink and she looked away from him, staring back at the house as if longing to run inside and escape him. "It was that night that I realized I just wasn't ready for this…for you."

"And when will you be ready? Because I'll wait. Ask around town, Jewel. People will tell you I'm a very patient man, especially when it comes to something…someone I think is important."

She looked up at him again and in the depths of her chocolate eyes he saw a yearning and he knew for certain that they were worth fighting for. All he had to figure out was exactly what he was fighting against.

"If we moved too fast, we can slow things down," he continued. "I'll take you out to dinner. We can see a movie and I won't touch you, won't kiss you again unless you give me express permission."

A half laugh, half sob escaped her. "Oh, Quinn, you're making things so difficult. That's why I didn't want to talk to you—because I knew you wouldn't just accept what I said without question."

"I accept things when they make sense, but so far you haven't told me anything that makes sense." He placed a hand on her shoulder. "The other night was amazing and confirmed for me that you're the woman I've been waiting for all this time. I thought I could be the man you were waiting for, too."

She stepped away from his touch, as if finding it painful and that only confirmed his feeling that she cared about him and was running away from him for another reason.

"Talk to me, Jewel. Tell me what's really going on." He'd thought he'd never find love again when Sarah died. He'd believed all chance of happiness had died with his wife.

But after spending time with Jewel, after making love to her, he knew she was his second chance for happiness and he wasn't about to let her walk away without an explanation that made sense.

She straightened her shoulders but her gaze didn't quite meet his. "You're a nice man, Quinn. And I got caught up in the moment with you, but I'm just not ready for any relationship with a man. I'm sorry if I led you on, but there's nothing else to say."

She didn't wait for his response, but rather turned

and headed toward the house with Cocoa running at her side.

Quinn watched her go, his heart a leaden weight in the pit of his stomach.

Quinn had never been an egotistical man, but he didn't believe her. He didn't believe that she'd gotten caught up in the moment and now realized she didn't care about him. When he'd touched her, he'd seen a flare of desire in her eyes. She wanted him still.

Jewel Mayfair had secrets. He'd sensed that since the moment he'd met her and he was determined to get to the bottom of things, to discover the secrets that kept her from a life of happiness with him.

## Chapter 9

The night wrapped around Jewel like a lover with a fever, the heat of the day maintaining its grip long after night had fallen.

She'd spent the last two hours tossing and turning in bed, unable to find sleep no matter how hard she tried. She'd finally given up and decided to take a walk in the woods.

This time it wasn't ghostly voices or baby cries that had kept her from falling asleep. Rather, it had been thoughts of Quinn.

Seeing him that morning had been far more difficult than she'd thought it would be. Telling him she didn't want a relationship with him had been sheer torture. All she'd really wanted to do was rush into his arms, hear his deep, reassuring voice telling her that they were going to have a wonderful future together.

But as long as she questioned her own sanity, she would never allow herself to be with any man who would have to go through with her what she'd lived through in the final months of her mother's life.

It had taken her years to connect with Patsy and even though the Baylors had raised her with love, she'd needed something from her mother that they hadn't been able to give her. Unfortunately, she'd never gotten it. Patsy had been incapable of giving love to the daughter she rarely recognized and could no longer remember giving birth to.

It had to be like what family members of Alzheimer's patients went through and Jewel wouldn't consciously choose to put somebody she loved through that.

The brush rustled to her left and she caught her breath in surprise. Slowly she breathed again as she realized she must have disturbed some poor creature's slumber. Nice that somebody could get some sleep tonight, she thought ruefully.

Even though she was dressed only in her night-gown and a lightweight short robe, the heat was oppressive, pressing in on her from all sides. There had been a number of power outages over the last couple of days due to the heat and the overload on the electrical grid. And there was no break in sight.

She heard a rustling from someplace behind her. She froze again. It hadn't sounded like a little night creature. It had sounded big. The sound came again, this time a little closer, a loud crashing as if something or someone was running toward her.

She thought of all those times she'd felt as if somebody was watching her and a lump of apprehension jumped into her throat. A burst of adrenaline shot through her and then came the taste of fear.

As the noise grew closer, she ran blindly down the narrow path, her heart pounding. She threw a glance over her shoulders and although she saw nothing on the path behind her, she saw movement in the tangled woods and brush just off the path.

There was no question in her mind. Somebody was after her and the fact that he hadn't said a word, was rushing at her out of the dark, terrified her.

She was afraid to run full tilt on the dark path. If she banged into a tree or tripped over an exposed root, then whoever was behind her would catch her. If she ran fast enough and far enough, she'd eventually reach Clay's place and safety, but the crashing noise let her know that whoever was chasing her was getting closer.

Tears filled her eyes, making vision even more difficult. She tripped and painfully smashed a knee to the ground. She scrambled back to her feet and kept moving, a sob escaping her lips.

"Jewel?" The deep voice boomed from just ahead of her.

She sobbed in relief as Quinn appeared on the path in front of her. His tall, lean silhouette in the near-darkness appeared like an island in a sea of shark-infested waters. She didn't hesitate but ran directly into his arms. "S-Somebody chasing me." Her teeth chattered despite the warmth of the night.

He tightened his arms around her. "It's okay. You're safe now."

She hid her face in the front of his clean-smelling shirt and after a moment had passed she didn't hear any noise except the beating of her own heart, and the beating of his. Here was safety, in his big, strong arms.

Looking up at him, she saw his gaze taking in the woods around them, felt the slight tension that filled his body, the tension of a man ready to fight whatever might crawl out of the darkness. It only made her feel even safer.

"I don't see or hear anything," he finally said. "Whatever it was or whoever it was is gone. Come on, I'll walk you back to your house," he said as she finally stepped away from him.

He took her by the arm, as if to keep her close to him as they began to walk back to the ranch. She welcomed his touch, the reassuring feel of his warm hand on her arm. "Why don't you have Cocoa with you?" he asked.

"I was afraid he'd bark at everything that moved and disturb the kids," she replied. With each step she took with Quinn at her side, her heartbeat slowed to a more normal pace.

"Quinn, I didn't imagine it. There was somebody

chasing me," she said as they left the path and entered the gate that led into the pool area.

In the moonlight his gaze held surprise as he looked at her. "It never entered my mind that you imagined it," he said. He motioned her toward one of the pool chairs. "Let's sit for a minute, let you calm down before you go inside."

The idea of sitting and talking to him was much more appealing that her going back to her bedroom alone with only her thoughts as company. She sat in a chair and Quinn next to her, close enough that she could smell his familiar scent.

"Better?" he asked after a minute of silence.

"I was better the minute you appeared on that path," she confessed.

He leaned forward and took one of her hands in his. "I get the feeling that there are things you aren't telling me and I wish I could make you realize that it's okay to trust me. I don't want to give up on you, Jewel. Nothing you said to me makes me believe we can't have a future together."

She felt as if her heart were being ripped in half. "Did you know I lost a baby?" The words tumbled from her lips before they had fully formed in her head.

He drew in an audible breath and his hand tightened on hers. "No, I didn't know that."

"It was in the accident that killed Andrew. I was four months' pregnant when I left the restaurant with Andrew that night. Then the accident happened and I was knocked unconscious. When I regained consciousness the next morning, both Andrew and my baby were gone."

"I'm sorry, Jewel. I'm so damned sorry for you."

The grief in his voice oddly enough eased some of her own. *Tell him about the cries,* a little voice whispered inside her. *Tell him that you hear Andrew calling your name during the night.*

But she didn't. She couldn't. What if he told somebody else and word got out that Jewel Mayfair was unbalanced, that she heard and saw ghosts in the night. She would lose her position here at the ranch, and that, along with the children here, were all that kept her from utter despair.

"Jewel, I know that what you went through was horrible and there will always be a place in your heart for all you lost, but isn't there a place for me, as well?"

Again a new pain ripped through her as she gazed into his beautiful eyes, felt the warmth and caring radiating from his hand holding hers.

"You're too young a woman to allow grief to forever rule your heart. There can be other babies. You can have a life filled with love." He leaned back a bit. "Maybe what you're suffering is a bit of Kelsey-itis," he continued.

She frowned. "What do you mean?"

"You're desperately afraid to grab on to happiness again because you know that it can be stolen away. You told me that you've told her that you need to grab on to it when it comes and hold tight so that you at least have memories of happiness if it goes away.

Maybe you need to take your own advice. You need to let go of Andrew to make room for new happiness."

Was it possible that the voice and the cries of a baby were nothing more than her trying to keep Andrew and that distant happiness alive? Was it possible that in embracing what Quinn offered, in allowing him into her heart, the cries from the grave would finally be silenced forever?

For the first time since arriving in Esperanza, her heart filled with a fragile hope. She wanted to reach out to Quinn. She wanted him in her life.

"We can take it slow, Jewel," he said. "We can take it as slow as you want. I know you have a lot of things on your mind right now with Joe and Meredith coming to town next weekend and I realize your job here takes up a lot of your time. I'll take whatever you can give me. Just don't cut me out."

"I don't want to cut you out," she said softly, and this time it was she who tightened her grip on his hand. "Maybe I *have* been afraid to let go of the past," she admitted slowly.

"Trust me, I understand. After Sarah died, I grieved for a long time. I was afraid that if I let go of the grief I'd have nothing, be nothing. It defined me for a long time. Then one morning I woke up and the sun was shining and the birds were singing and I decided I wouldn't let my grief define me for another moment. It was time to start living again."

"Have you ever thought about being a psychologist?" she asked teasingly.

He laughed, that low, deep sound that wrapped around her heart and warmed her from the inside out. "I have enough problems figuring out the psychological problems of animals. I wouldn't attempt to try to analyze people. I'll leave that to you." He released her hand. "Now why don't you try to get some sleep?"

She nodded and stood. As always she found Quinn a rock of steadiness, a source of calm that she welcomed. He walked with her to her back door then he took her in his arms and she stepped into the embrace.

"If I call you tomorrow, will you take my call or at least return it if you're out?" he asked.

"Absolutely," she replied. What he'd said about her being a lot like Kelsey had made sense. She was willing, at least for now, to reach out for happiness, reach out to him and see where the path led.

"And if I invited you to have lunch one day this week?"

"I think we could arrange something like that," she replied.

"Good." His eyes gleamed and he pressed a kiss to her forehead. "Then I'll just say∆ good night."

"Good night Quinn," she replied. She watched as he went back to the gate and then disappeared into the darkness of the night.

She went inside and hoped she wasn't making a mistake. Maybe the haunting she'd been experiencing since arriving here was simply her mind refusing to let go of the past. Perhaps now that she'd made a decision to go forward, leaving her past behind, the haunting would stop.

It wasn't until she was back in bed that she realized that one question hadn't been answered. Who had been chasing her through the woods?

"It's looking good," Jewel said to Ryder the next morning. The pen was almost complete and the kids had spent most of breakfast discussing what kind of animals they'd like to have.

Barry had wanted a hippo and Lindy had her heart set on a baby elephant. It had taken some fast talking to bring them back to reality.

Ryder wiped a handkerchief across his sweaty brow. "We should have it finished in the next day or two."

"Terrific. I'm heading into town. Is there anything you need?" she asked.

"No, I'm good." He picked up his hammer. "I think the kids have the right idea today."

Jeff and Cheryl had the kids out by the pool. The sounds of splashing and laughter rode on the hot, steamy air. "Feel free to join them," Jewel said. "I think they plan on being out there all afternoon. In the meantime, I'm off. I'm meeting Ellie to talk about the plans for next Sunday."

"Have fun," he replied.

Minutes later, as Jewel drove into town, her mind whirled with all the things she needed to check out with Ellie. Weeks ago, when she'd first found out that

Joe and Meredith intended to stop here on the final leg of their campaign trail, she'd spoken with Ellie about a tent rental, chairs and tables and all the functional things that were needed to accommodate a big crowd. Today she wanted to discuss the menu.

As she thought of seeing Joe and Meredith again, her heart filled with joy. When Jewel had learned about her real mother and had found Patsy in the mental ward, Patsy had told her of her other two children, Joe and Teddy. Patsy had said she never knew the identity of her first son's father and had hinted that Teddy's father was a member of Joe's family.

Jewel hadn't known what to believe or whether she would be welcome into the Colton family after all that her mother had done. But Joe and Meredith had opened their loving arms to her and embraced her as one of their own. With Patsy gone and her adoptive parents also deceased, Joe and Meredith had become like parents to her.

It was Meredith's loving support that had gotten Jewel through those dark days after the accident, and it was Meredith who had given her a new start here in Esperanza.

Jewel couldn't wait to see them both again and she wanted everything perfect for their visit. She wanted to prove to her aunt Meredith that trusting Jewel with the Hopechest Ranch had been the right thing to do.

Ellie's shop was on Main Street, a tiny storefront with artificial flower arrangements, wooden trellises and a champagne fountain for rent in the windows.

"Ellie?" Jewel cried out as she entered the shop.

"I'm back here." Ellie's voice drifted out from the back room. "I'll be right out."

Jewel sat in the chair in front of the desk and waited for Ellie. The store was a fantasyland of party supplies and Jewel never tired of looking around.

Ellie appeared, her brown frizzy hair looking wilder than usual and her cheeks flushed a bright pink. "Sorry, I was getting things together for a wedding that's taking place tomorrow. I swear, something's in the air around here lately. I've never been so busy." She flopped down at her desk and blew a strand of her hair out of her eyes. She grinned. "Now, let's talk about your big deal next Sunday."

For the next hour they went over the menu and checked and rechecked the lists of things that Ellie and her crew would be providing for the day.

"Your guests are arriving around five, right?" Ellie asked. Jewel nodded and Ellie continued. "My crew will be at your place no later than ten in the morning to start setting things up."

It was after two when Jewel left Ellie's. The heat slammed her in the face as she walked out of the cool store and she was eager to get back to the house and maybe join the kids in the pool. With this heat, no other place sounded the least bit attractive.

As she walked to her car she got that feeling again, the prickly sensation of somebody watching her, of something not quite right. She glanced around, seeking the source of the odd feeling.

Although there were other people on the side-walks, nobody was paying any attention to her. They were hurrying toward stores, going about their lives.

She dismissed the feeling and got into her car, relieved as she drove away to see nobody following her.

An hour later Jewel was in her modest one-piece bathing suit and playing a game of water volleyball with the kids. Jeff and Cheryl sat in the shade of one of the umbrella tables, Cheryl calling out encouragement.

It was right before dinner that Jewel thought about Jeff Cookson. He was a quiet man, good with the kids, but he always appeared vaguely uncomfortable when interacting with Jewel.

Was it possible that it had been Jeff who had chased her through the woods the night before? Before hiring the couple, who were originally from San Antonio, where they had worked at a juvenile facility, Jewel had checked and double-checked their references and found them impeccable.

She dismissed the idea of Jeff skulking around after her in the dead of night, but that left her with the question that had plagued her since she'd awakened that morning. Who had been in the woods with her?

After dinner Jewel and the children had a group therapy session in the playroom. She talked to the kids about good and bad emotions and the appropriate way to express them. They followed up the session with a movie and then it was bedtime.

With the house quiet and at rest, Jewel curled up

in bed with a book. She'd only been reading a few minutes when the phone rang.

"Good day?" Quinn's deep voice washed over her and she smiled with the simple pleasure of hearing it.

"Great day," she replied. "I finalized things with Ellie for the barbecue on Sunday and spent the rest of the day in the pool and doing therapy with the kids. What about you?"

"I operated on a dog with kidney stones, checked out a horse that had rubbed a sore spot on her flank and spent the rest of the day reading the books I got from the library the other day. It was just a normal day in the life of a small-town vet, a normal day made better now that I've heard your voice."

She smiled into the phone. "I feel the same way about hearing your voice. It's a perfect way to end the day."

"Are you ready for bed?" he asked.

"Actually, I'm in bed. I was just doing a little reading. The house is quiet and after all the fun in the sun this afternoon I actually feel like I'm going to be able to sleep."

"Good. Then I'll let you go. I just didn't want the day to pass without talking to you. Can you work me in for lunch one day this week?"

"Maybe Thursday would be good, but I'll have to let you know the first of the week." She had no idea what the week might bring with all the preparations for Joe and Meredith.

"Okay, I'll check in with you tomorrow or Monday. Good night, Jewel, and sweet dreams."

As she hung up, a pleasurable warmth remained. If she let herself she could easily fall in love with Quinn Logan. She was already more than halfway there. She just wasn't sure if she should allow herself to take the full leap.

Yawning with sleepiness, she turned out her lamp and got settled for the night. As she fell asleep she filled her head with thoughts of Quinn, of how it felt to be held in his arms, how endearing it was when he shoved that mane of beautiful hair away from his eyes.

There was something so solid about him, a quiet confidence that made her believe he could handle anything life might throw his way. He'd gotten through both the death of his wife and the damage to his professional reputation with dignity and grace. She fell asleep remembering the feel of his warm lips against hers.

She jerked awake abruptly and sat up, unsure what had pulled her from a dreamless sleep. A glance at the clock told her it was just after two.

Her heart pounded unnaturally fast and she wasn't sure why. Had it been a dream that had awoken her? A nightmare she now couldn't remember?

Maybe a glass of water would calm her racing heart. She slid her legs over the side of the mattress and reached for her robe at the end of her bed. She didn't need her bedside lamp to make her way to the kitchen. The path was lit with nightlights in case one of the kids got up and wandered in the night.

She'd just reached the doorway into the living room when she heard it—the sound of several heavy footsteps coming from the family room/kitchen area.

Her heart leapt into her throat. Those footsteps didn't belong to one of the children, nor would Jeff or Cheryl be wandering the house in a heavy pair of shoes at this hour of the night.

She slid back into her bedroom and grabbed the bat she kept near her bed. With this being a ranch for children she refused to have a gun, but at this moment she wished she were holding something more lethal than a baseball bat.

If there was an intruder in the house, her sole concern was for the safety of her charges. Gripping the wooden weapon tightly in both hands, she advanced through the living room. She stifled a small gasp as she passed the front door and saw it cracked open.

Somebody was in the house!

Somebody who didn't belong.

Her mind whirled a thousand miles a minute as she crept forward, searching the shadows of the room for potential danger.

When they'd first opened the ranch, there had been some people who weren't thrilled at the idea of a place for troubled kids here. Had somebody who had a problem decided to act on it?

From the living room she walked to the doorway that led to the family room and kitchen area. Her heart hammered so hard in her chest that she felt as if she might pass out. She kept the bat on her shoulders, ready to hit a home run if it became necessary. Her eyes had adjusted to the near-darkness of the house.

She saw nobody in the family room and was beginning to think that maybe whoever had been inside was now gone. She had no idea what they might have been looking for or what they'd been doing, but a tiny edge of relief whispered through her. She relaxed her grip on the bat handle.

Turning, she looked into the darkened kitchen and froze, every nerve and muscle screaming inside her as she saw the tall, dark form of a man. She must have made a noise for he turned to face her, his features covered by the dark material of a ski mask.

"Who are you? What do you want?" The words barely escaped her lips before he rushed toward her.

## Chapter 10

Everything seemed to move in slow motion. His heavy footsteps rang on the floor as he came toward her. She gripped the bat tightly and swung.

Strike.

She missed him and stumbled backward. *Three strikes and you're out,* she thought as she fought back a wild, hysterical burst of terrified giggles. But the giggles died a quick death as he once again advanced toward her and tried to grab her by the throat.

She ducked and evaded his grasp, her heart hammering with flight-or-fight adrenaline. She tried to discern his features beneath the ski mask, desperately looking for something familiar, a clue to his identity, but she couldn't even tell the color of his eyes in the narrow slits.

She didn't have to know his identity to recognize that he was dangerous. She could sense an evil intent wafting from his big body. A scream rose to her lips but she fought it back, bit it away. The last thing she wanted was to scream and have one of the children stumble sleepily into the room.

He growled, like a wild animal let loose after months of captivity. The ominous sound raised the hairs on the nape of her neck, washed through her a terror she'd never known.

As he rushed toward her again, she swung the bat wildly and felt the whomph of it connecting with some part of his body. He grunted in obvious pain then pushed her to the side so hard she crashed to the floor. He ran past her and out the front door.

Jewel scrambled to her feet, ignoring the pain in her hip from the fall. Once again with the bat held ready to hit a home run, she advanced toward the open front door.

Her heart hammered.

Was he there?

Just outside? Waiting for her to run after him? Heart pounding so hard she could hear it banging in her brain, she moved closer. When she reached the door, she slammed it closed and locked it, then leaned weakly against it as a sob choked out of her.

Who was he? What had he wanted? She needed to call somebody. Sheriff Yates. She had to report this. She shoved away from the door and immediately turned on all the lights in the family room. Deep tremors possessed her as she stumbled toward the telephone on the end table.

It took her shaking fingers two tries to finally punch in the right numbers and connect with the dispatcher for the sheriff's office. She told him she needed somebody out here, that there'd been an intruder in the house. "And no lights or sirens," she exclaimed. The dispatcher told her somebody would be out as soon as possible.

She hung up the receiver and leaned back, the bat still clutched tightly in one hand. What would have happened if she hadn't had the bat? She didn't even want to think about it.

Was the man who had been inside the house tonight the same one who had chased her through the woods? Was he the one she'd sensed watching her?

There had been such rage in that growl he'd released. He'd been like a marauding bear, who wanted nothing more than to rip her limb from limb.

She shivered and rose on shaky legs to go to the front window and watch for Jericho Yates or Adam. Was the intruder still out there? Hiding in the night? Waiting for another opportunity? She checked the lock on the front door, making sure it was engaged.

How had he gotten in? Was it possible the front door had been left unlocked when they'd all gone to bed? She frowned and tried to remember if she'd locked it or not. She just couldn't be sure.

She was vaguely surprised that nobody had heard anything, but then she realized that the assault had all been relatively silent. Other than those initial few words that she'd spoken aloud when she'd first seen him and that horrible low growl, there had been little noise.

She breathed a small prayer of thanks that none of the children had awakened. Not only could they have been physically harmed, but it was vital to their mental well-being for them to believe that they were safe and secure here in their temporary home.

It seemed like an eternity before she saw a car coming down the road. When the vehicle turned into the driveway she saw that it was from the sheriff's office.

The car parked in front and as the door opened she recognized Adam. As he got out of the car she unlocked the front door and opened it to meet him.

"Are you all right?" he asked as he reached her, concern darkening his eyes.

She nodded, for a moment too overwhelmed to speak. Hot tears burned at her eyes, rose up in the back of her throat. Now that she knew she was safe she realized that she was precariously close to breaking down.

Adam gripped her arm tightly. "Is somebody still inside?"

"No." She finally found her voice. "No, he ran out the front door."

"Go back inside. Lock the door. I'm going to do

a sweep of the area and I'll be back in a few minutes to talk to you."

She nodded, closed the door and relocked it. Her heartbeat was slowing to a more normal pace and some of the trembling that had possessed her body had finally stilled.

Standing by the window, she saw Adam's flashlight as he searched the front yard. He disappeared from sight around the side of the house and she drew a deep breath to steady her racing emotions.

Although it soothed her to know that Adam was out looking, she didn't expect him to stumble upon the intruder. He was probably long gone…and hopefully with a cracked rib or a broken leg to boot.

What she'd like to do was pick up the phone and call Quinn. She knew the sound of his deep, calm voice would anchor her, soothe her. But she wouldn't wake him in the middle of the night, hated herself for her weakness in needing him, wanting him.

"Jewel?"

She gasped and whirled around to see Cheryl standing behind her, her robe clutched closed, brown hair in sleep disarray and her eyes wide in alarm. "You scared me to death," Jewel exclaimed.

"Sorry. What's going on?" She eyed the bat that Jewel had refused to release.

"Somebody was in the house. A man. He tried to attack me but I hit him with the bat and he ran out the door. Deputy Rawlings is here now, checking out the area."

"Oh my God." Cheryl moved closer to Jewel. "Are you sure you're okay?" Jewel nodded. "Do you know who it was? What he wanted?"

"I don't have a clue," Jewel replied.

"How did he get in?"

"By the front door." Jewel frowned. "I can't remember if I locked it before I went to bed or not."

At that moment a soft knock sounded at the door. Jewel opened it to allow Adam inside. "Unfortunately, I didn't find anything," he said.

"Let's go into the kitchen," Jewel suggested. She finally let go of the bat, leaning it against the family-room wall. "I'd rather not wake the children."

With Jewel leading the way, they filed into the kitchen area. "This is where I first saw him," Jewel said. "I'm not sure what woke me up, but I thought I heard the sound of footsteps and I grabbed the bat and I saw him."

Cheryl placed a comforting arm around Jewel's shoulders. "You should have called to us. You should have called for Jeff."

"Where is Jeff?" Adam asked.

Cheryl gave them a sheepish expression. "He's still asleep. But if you would have screamed, he would have woken up."

"I didn't want to scream," Jewel replied. "The last thing I wanted was one of the kids waking up and coming into the room."

"Did you recognize him? Did he say anything to you?" Adam asked.

"No, nothing. He had on a ski mask. I didn't recognize him and he didn't say anything to me."

"What about height and weight?" Adam pulled out a small notepad from his shirt pocket.

For the next few minutes Jewel described her assailant, although there was precious little she could tell him. Adam made a sweep of the house, then there was nothing more he could do. "It sounds to me like you probably interrupted a robbery," Adam said.

Jewel nodded. "I think you're right. He probably wouldn't have tried to attack me if I hadn't confronted him." She wanted to believe this. It was the only thing that made sense.

It was after three when she walked with Adam out on the porch. "I'd like to tell you that I'm certain we'll catch this guy, but with the sketchy information you gave me, I don't have a good feeling about it," Adam said. "I'll check with the local doctors to see if anyone shows up with broken ribs or unusual bruising, but the man would be a fool to do that unless you seriously hurt him."

Jewel sighed and tied the belt of her robe more tightly around her. "I hope I busted his spleen," she exclaimed as she wrapped her arms around herself to ward off an inner chill.

"Jewel, I could stay the night if it would make you feel better," he said. He moved to stand next to her and put his hand on her forearm. "You should know by now that there's nothing I'd like more than to have a permanent place here at the ranch with you and the kids."

She realized it was time to be truthful with the handsome deputy. From the moment he'd arrived in town he'd made it clear to her that he wanted a relationship with her. It was time he knew the truth.

"Adam, you're a wonderful man and I'm sure someday you'll make somebody a great husband, but that somebody won't be me. I like you. I like you a lot and I hope we can remain friends, but I just don't feel that way about you. I'm sorry."

He dropped his hand from her arm and stepped back from her, a look of disappointment crossing his features. "No need to apologize. If it's not there, it's not there. I can't say I'm not disappointed, but I also can't say I'm surprised." He offered her a smile. "If we'd both been on the same page, we would have been dating for the last couple of months."

He jammed his hands into his pockets. "I'll let you know what I find out in the next day or two about what went on here tonight. Take care of yourself, Jewel, and if you ever change your mind you know where to find me."

She watched from the door as he walked to his car and got in. She had a feeling there would be fewer impromptu check-ins by him in the future now that he knew there was no hope for them.

When she returned to the kitchen, Cheryl had made a pot of hot tea and sat at the table. "Come on, have a cup of tea. I know well enough that you probably won't sleep for the rest of the night." Cheryl got up and fixed her a cup of tea, then put it on the table.

Jewel sat down wearily. Now that the excitement was over and Adam was gone, she was aware of the throb of her hip and a headache pounding at her temples. "Thanks," she said and cupped her hands around the warmth of the cup.

"Are you sure you're okay?" Cheryl asked as she gazed at Jewel with concern.

"I'm fine. I just have a headache." She took a sip of the tea, hoping the hot liquid would ease some of the pain in her head. "I just wish I knew why that man was inside, what he wanted here."

"Maybe it was a local kid who thought you had psychiatric drugs," Cheryl offered.

"Maybe, but if it was a kid, he was definitely a big kid. I just don't want anything to happen to mess up the big barbecue next Sunday," Jewel said worriedly.

"Don't worry, everything will be fine for Joe and Meredith's visit," Cheryl assured her.

"I hope so." Jewel took another sip of the tea, welcoming the warmth that helped banished the chill that had been with her since the moment she'd opened her eyes and realized something wasn't right in the house.

"Is there anything else I can do for you?" Cheryl asked.

"Yes, go back to bed," Jewel replied with a tired smile.

"Are you sure? I don't mind sitting with you if you want me to."

"No, I'm fine. I'm just going to finish this cup of tea then I'm going back to bed myself. Wait, I changed my mind, there *is* something you can do for me. Would you wait by the front door while I go get Cocoa? I think it's time our furry friend moved from the garage into the house." Jewel got up from her chair and carried her teacup to the sink.

"Sounds like a good idea," Cheryl agreed. "I doubt that dog would bite anyone, but if somebody comes in who doesn't belong he could sure raise a ruckus by barking."

Jewel stopped in the family room to grab her bat, then Cheryl followed her to the front door, where Jewel grabbed the leash hanging on a hook by the door and flipped on the outside light. As she stepped onto the porch, her heart began to bang with apprehension.

Was the man who'd been inside out here lingering in the night? Had he watched from some safe place while Adam searched for him, then left? It suddenly seemed like a long trip between the house and the garages.

"If you see anything or anyone, scream like hell," she said to Cheryl.

"Don't worry. And trust me, I can scream loud enough they'll hear me in town."

Jewel nodded. With the bat gripped in one hand and the leash in the other, she began the long walk toward the garage.

The night was silent and she listened for any sound that might forewarn her of anything amiss, but she arrived at the garage door without incident.

It took only moments to fasten Cocoa's leash then hurry back to the house where Cheryl waited at the front door. Cocoa danced with excitement, obviously thrilled to have his sleep interrupted by human interaction. He had lavished her with kisses as she connected the leash, then pranced next to her as they went back to the house.

"Thanks, Cheryl," she said once they were back inside with the door locked securely behind them. "I'll see you in the morning."

Jewel was thankful that Cocoa didn't bark as she led him to her quarters and closed the door behind them. She took the leash off him and he ran around the room, sniffing every corner and huffing with excitement.

Jewel set the bat against the wall next to her bed, then took off her robe. She was certain she wouldn't get any more sleep, but her aching body yearned for the softness of her mattress.

As she got into bed, Cocoa jumped up next to her and curled up as if he'd spent every night of his life sleeping in the bed with her.

"Don't get used to that," she said to him. "Tomorrow we'll bring in your bed."

He hunkered down and released what could only be described as a deliriously happy sigh. Jewel reached out a hand and stroked his soft fur. The feel reminded her of Quinn's hair, soft and silky to the touch.

As she continued to stroke the dog, she felt her heartbeat slowing and her tension ebbing. It had to have been a botched robbery attempt.

Although the attack had felt personal when he'd emitted that growl and had reached to grab her around the neck, surely it hadn't been personal at all. She'd trapped him and, like a wild animal, he'd sprung to get free.

She'd made no enemies that she knew of since coming to Esperanza. Some of the townspeople hadn't initially been thrilled with the idea of a ranch for troubled kids in their midst, but the last couple of months of the ranch's smooth running had quieted even the most vocal of critics.

Even though she had no intention of falling asleep, she must have, for she awakened to Cocoa licking her arm. A glance at her clock let her know it was a few minutes before seven, time to get up and face a new day.

"Okay, just a minute," she said to Cocoa, who jumped off the bed and began to run in circles near her closed bedroom door. "I'm hurrying." She got out of bed and pulled on her robe, afraid that Cocoa's obvious need to go outside wouldn't wait until she showered and dressed for the day.

She fastened the leash on his collar, then opened her bedroom door. The scent of freshly brewed coffee and frying bacon greeted her. Cocoa stopped in his tracks and sniffed the air, momentarily distracted from his run to the front door by the delicious scent.

"Come on, boy. First things first," she said as she tugged him toward the door. Once she was at the door, she released his leash and let him run while she stood in the yard and watched. He disappeared around the side of the garage and was gone for a minute or two, then came running back to her.

"Good boy," she said. "Cocoa is a good boy." She patted his neck, then reattached the leash and led him to the garage.

She had quickly discovered that having him in the house while the kids got ready for school was too much of a distraction. He chased the children and barked for them to play with him while they were trying to get dressed.

Once the kids were on the bus, she'd let him back into the house. After last night, she was determined to acclimate him quickly to being inside rather than in the confines of the garage.

Returning to her quarters, she showered and dressed for the day and by the time she got to the kitchen the kids were up and the house was filled with the usual chaos of morning.

Once the kids had left for the day, Jewel returned to the kitchen for another cup of coffee. Jeff sat at the table with her while Cheryl bustled around, clearing the last of the breakfast dishes.

"Cheryl told me about what I slept through last night," Jeff said, his hazel eyes narrowed in concern. "I can't believe you tried to take on an intruder by yourself."

"In the light of day I can't believe it myself," Jewel admitted, a coldness seeping through her as she thought of those terrifying moments the night before.

"The only good thing is that I managed to hit him hard enough to hurt."

"Still, what good is it to have a man in the house if you don't holler for him when you need him?" Jeff replied gruffly.

Cheryl turned from the sink and grinned at Jewel. "He's having a hero meltdown this morning. He wanted to be the hero and instead you took care of the situation yourself."

"Trust me, if something like that ever happens again, I'll scream," Jewel said. "Thank goodness it was a case of all's well that ends well."

"Maybe Deputy Rawlings will be able to figure out who it was," Cheryl said.

"Probably some kid looking for drugs," Jeff replied.

"That's what I think," Jewel agreed. "He probably thought he could find some good psychiatric drugs in the house."

"On another topic, we're still on to take the kids Saturday for that field trip, right?" Jeff asked.

"Absolutely. That will work perfectly with me. While y'all are gone I'm going to clean this place from top to bottom to have it ready for the barbecue on Sunday." Jewel finished her coffee and stood. "And now I'm going to go get Cocoa and let him back in here. I also want to move his bed from the garage to my bedroom. From now on he'll be in the house at night."

"Need any help?" Jeff asked.

"No, thanks. I can take care of it," she replied.

"Then I'm going to do a little yard work before it gets too hot to breathe outside." Jeff pushed his chair away from the table and stood. "And if my wife loves me, she'll bring me out something cold to drink in the next hour or so."

Cheryl smiled at him and for a moment Jewel felt like a third wheel as she sensed the love radiating between the two.

As she walked outside to the garage, a deep yearning slid through her and her head filled with thoughts of Quinn. She felt as if she were being selfish in pursuing a relationship with him and not telling him about the voices she heard at night, the haunting cry of a baby that made her doubt her own sanity.

But the idea of not grasping on to the happiness he brought into her life was devastating. All her words of wisdom to Kelsey would mean nothing if she didn't embrace the philosophy of reaching out for happiness herself.

She opened the side garage door and stepped inside Cocoa's temporary quarters, expecting to be met as usual with a tail wag and a tongue lavishing, but Cocoa didn't greet her at the door.

He lay on the floor in a pool of vomit. As he saw her he struggled to stand, but his legs buckled and he collapsed back to the floor.

"Oh my God," she cried, and whirled to the door. "Jeff! Come quick. Something is wrong with Cocoa." Her heart leapt into her throat as she crouched down beside the dog. Tears washed from her eyes. "It's okay, baby. You're going to be all right. We just need to get you to Quinn's."

She stood as Jeff entered. "He was fine this morning," she said.

"Definitely not fine now," Jeff said with grim expression.

"Let's get him loaded in the car and take him to Quinn's."

They used a worn blanket and wrapped Cocoa up in it, then placed him in the backseat of Jewel's car. "Want me to come with you?" Jeff asked as she started the engine.

"No. Stay here. I'll let you know what's going on." She didn't take time to say anything more, but quickly tore down the driveway and onto the road to Quinn's.

She kept up a steady stream of chatter as she drove, unsure if she were trying to calm herself or the dog. "Quinn will take care of you. It's going to be okay." It was shocking to her how quickly the dog had crawled into her heart and she knew how deeply he'd already ingrained himself into the hearts of the children.

He had to be okay. He just had to be! She roared down the highway and breathed a sigh of relief as she turned into Quinn's place.

Quinn's house sat back from the road, an attractive ranch-style house with hunter-green shutters. But she pulled in front of the building closest to the road and parked. That one-story building was where Quinn's veterinary practice was housed.

Hank Webster, a local rancher was just leaving as she got out of her car. "Please, could you help me? I've got a very sick dog and I need help getting him inside."

With Hank's help they managed to get Cocoa inside where Quinn's receptionist, Brenda Lopez, quickly gestured them into an examining room.

With Cocoa on the table, Jewel thanked Hank, who then left. She stroked Cocoa's head and frowned as she smelled the strong scent of garlic emanating from the dog's breath.

"It's okay, boy," she said as tears misted her vision.

He whined, a pathetic little noise that broke her heart. What was wrong with him? What had happened? He'd been fine two hours ago.

She turned as the door to the room opened. Quinn walked in, one leg dragging in an unmistakable limp. He flashed her a quick smile. "What happened?" he asked as he went directly to Cocoa.

"I…I don't know." A chill swept through her, one that had nothing to do with worry for Cocoa. "What happened to your leg?" Her voice felt as if it came from someplace very far away.

"Molly the horse not only managed to tear up my face, she also got me in the knee. It sometimes acts up." He leaned closer to Cocoa's face. "Smell that garlicky scent. That's arsenic poisoning. I need to get him treated. Why don't you wait out in the waiting room?" He ushered her out then called for his vet tech to come into the room to help him.

On wooden legs she moved to one of the chairs

and sank down, her worry for Cocoa momentarily banished from her mind.

She felt blindsided. Last night she'd struck some-body in the lower body with a bat and today Quinn had a pronounced limp. There was no way to escape the icy chill that swept through her as she wondered if it had been Quinn in her house the night before.

She desperately wanted to believe that it was noth-ing more than a coincidence, but all she wanted to do was run and escape from him and from the terrible possibility that it had been his knee she'd hit the night before, that it had been his hands reaching for her throat.

# Chapter 11

Jewel felt as if she might throw up. An hour later as she drove home, her head whirled and nausea rolled in her stomach.

Cocoa had been poisoned with arsenic and Quinn had a mysterious limp. Any trust she'd felt toward the handsome vet had been shattered, leaving her feeling sick and making her realize just how much she cared about him.

She'd been more than half in love with him and given just a little more time she would have allowed herself to fall completely, head-over-heels. But the thought that she'd been the one who'd given him that injury with her bat filled her with coldness.

He'd managed to get Cocoa stabilized, but had

told her the dog needed to stay for a couple of days to make sure there were no residual effects from the poison. They decided he would keep the dog until after the barbecue on Sunday.

She deserved an Oscar for her performance with him. Even when the emergency was over and he'd asked her when they were going to be able to have lunch together, she'd managed to keep her cool and not betray that anything was wrong. She'd told him that until the barbecue was over, they could not get together. She simply had too much to do.

Thankfully he'd had an appointment with a sick cat and with a squeeze of her hand he'd told her they'd talk later. She hadn't been able to escape fast enough.

Tightening her grip on the steering wheel, she thought about that moment when she'd seen the intruder standing in her kitchen. Had he been as tall as Quinn? Were Quinn's shoulders as broad as that man's had been? It could have been Quinn beneath that ski mask.

By the time she reached her place, none of the questions had been answered and the sickness that had gripped her had only grown more intense.

Jeff greeted her as she parked the car. "I found part of a steak in Cocoa's part of the garage," he said when she got out of the car. "I think maybe your intruder left it for the dog."

She nodded. "Quinn said he thinks it was arsenic poisoning, so I guess that makes as much sense as anything right now."

"How's the dog?"

"Serious, but stable," she replied. "If you'll excuse me, I'm going to my room to clean up a bit."

Her intention was to shower again and change her clothes, which smelled like dog vomit. She had no intention of crying. But as she stripped and got beneath a hot spray of water, the tears began.

At first she thought she was crying for Cocoa, but as the tears increased she realized that she was weeping for what might have been with Quinn.

There was no going back. She would always wonder if he had been the man who had broken into the ranch, the man who had growled at her with such hatred, the one who had reached out to grab her around her throat.

Would Quinn, a man devoted to the health and well-being of animals, poison a dog? Why would he break into her house? What possible motive could he have? No matter how she twisted and turned the questions, she couldn't come up with any logical answers.

But she couldn't get that limp out of her mind. That physical injury of his had effectively killed any chance the two of them had for a future.

She refused to love a man she didn't trust. She leaned weakly against the shower stall and wept a lifetime of tears. She cried for the happiness she'd lost when Andrew and her baby had died. She sobbed for the happiness she might have found with Quinn. Finally, she cried because she didn't understand the twists and turns that life had thrown at her, beginning the day of her birth, when she'd been stolen away from her mother and sold in an illegal adoption.

The week passed in a haze for Jewel. She took care of the children, conducted therapy sessions and once again met with Ellie for the final preparations for Sunday's festivities.

Quinn called daily to update her on Cocoa's condition. They'd got the poison in time and Cocoa was doing just fine. She kept the conversation brief and light, although her heart had disengaged. She couldn't allow him back into her heart. She couldn't love him now, with all trust broken and a sliver of fear of him finding purchase in her heart.

It was just after nine on Saturday morning when Jeff and Cheryl rounded up the kids for their day trip away from the ranch.

"Make sure you all behave for Cheryl and Jeff," Jewel told each of the kids as they got into the minibus. "I want perfect behavior reports on each of you when you get home this evening."

"We'll be good," Barry promised, and they all echoed his words.

Although it was still early morning, the sun sizzled in a cloudless sky, promising no relief from the intense heat that had gripped the region for the past three days.

"Make sure they all get plenty to drink," Jewel said to Cheryl once they were all loaded and ready to pull away.

"Don't worry, Mother Hen. We'll bring your chicks home safe and sound," she assured Jewel.

Jewel forced a smile. "And call me if there are any problems," she said. She waved as they drove off and continued to wave and smile until the bus disappeared from sight.

Instantly her smile fell away. She was grateful that at least for the remainder of the day she wouldn't have to force a fake cheerfulness. She wouldn't have to pretend that everything was right in her world.

Sooner or later she was going to have to tell Quinn that there was no hope for them. The only reason she hadn't done so yet was because he would be attending the barbecue and she didn't want any unnecessary tension between them.

Once the barbecue was over and Joe and Meredith had left town, she'd tell Quinn that she wasn't available, that he needed to look elsewhere for a life partner.

The one thing she hadn't done was tell anyone about her suspicions. She'd considered calling Adam and telling him that Quinn was sporting a suspicious limp. The only thing that had stopped her was the possibility that Quinn might have been telling the truth about how his knee got injured.

Quinn had already lived through much of the town turning against him. He'd already faced false accusations that had nearly destroyed his life. She didn't want to be responsible for doing it all over again. She had no real proof, just a coincidental limp.

Just an awful limp that had destroyed everything.

As she stood there alone in the yard with the top of her head boiling beneath the hot sun, a sudden prickly feeling lifted the hair on the nape of her neck, raised goose bumps on her arms.

It was the crazy, inexplicable feeling a person got when she thought she was being watched. Jewel whirled around, eyeing the house behind her, then looked toward the nearby woods.

Nothing.

"Silly goose," she murmured to herself, but that didn't make the feeling go away. If she stood out here long enough, she would totally freak herself out.

She had a million and one things she wanted to accomplish today while the kids were out of the house. Standing in the front yard giving herself the heebie-jeebies wasn't on her to-do list. She headed inside and carefully locked the door behind her.

Although the children were responsible for cleaning their own rooms, Jewel wanted to give each room a thorough once-over. She knew there would be people with Joe and Meredith who had never been to the ranch before and would be looking closely at Meredith's pet project. Jewel wanted to make certain everything was perfect.

The morning passed quickly as she vacuumed and dusted each of the bedrooms, then tackled the bathrooms that the kids used.

The busywork kept her mind blank and for that she was grateful. Her brain felt fried from all the analyzing and thinking it had done over the past five days. She didn't want to think about anything but Joe and Meredith's visit the next day.

Not only would the day convene family and friends, it would also be an early celebration of Joe's political success. The polls and pundits were all forecasting a Colton presidency.

At noon Jewel stopped her work and sat at the table to enjoy a sandwich of the chicken salad Cheryl had fixed early that morning.

It was only as she sat eating that she realized just how quiet the house was with everyone gone. The silence pressed in on her from all sides. It wasn't a comfortable silence but rather an oppressive one.

And, as always when she had a moment of peace and her head was relatively empty, it filled with thoughts of Quinn. More than once she'd felt as if she were being watched. Was it possible Quinn had been stalking her long before they'd gotten close?

Had he merely stumbled on her that first night in the woods or had he been there all along, watching her? He'd known she often walked at night, had guessed that she suffered from insomnia.

She stifled a laugh of irony. She hadn't wanted to involve herself with him because she'd feared she was losing her mind. What if he was the one who was mentally deranged? An obsessed stalker, who had her in his sights?

Was it possible he had poisoned Cocoa with the intention of saving the dog and being a hero? The very idea sickened her.

She'd just finished eating and had put her dishes in the dishwasher when the doorbell rang. Grateful for a break in the silence and her racing thoughts, she hurried to answer.

She opened the door to Georgie and was ridiculously pleased to see the woman. "What a nice surprise!" she said as she opened the door to let her in.

"Nick and Emmie are having a bonding day. He took her to lunch and then was going to buy her a couple of pairs of new jeans for school. I was at loose ends so I thought I'd drop in and see if there's anything you need for tomorrow's big party."

"Come on in and have a glass of iced tea with me," Jewel said. "I think I have things under control for tomorrow. Ellie and her crew are going to arrive at ten in the morning to set up tents and chairs and everything we need to make the day a success."

As Georgie sat at the table, Jewel poured them each a glass of iced tea. "How does Emmie like school?" she asked as she joined Georgie.

"She loves it." Georgie's expression was a blend of happiness and wistfulness.

Jewel smiled. "Spoken with the bittersweet expression of a mother."

Georgie grinned. "She's already made friends with a bunch of kids and has assured me there isn't a cowboy in the bunch. She loves her teacher and she gets up every morning eager to go."

"And even though you want her to have friends and love school, it breaks your heart that she's expanding her horizons and doesn't need you quite as much as she did."

Georgie leaned back in her chair and sighed. "Exactly."

Jewel laughed. "Don't worry. You're still the most important thing in her world and will continue to be until she gets to be a teenager. Then she'll think you're the dumbest person on earth and wonder how you ever survived without her wisdom and knowledge."

Georgie laughed and shoved her long red braid over her shoulder. "God, I needed to hear that."

"How's Nick?"

"Bored. He's put in an application with the sheriff's office for a position as deputy, but so far there are no openings in the department. You can take the man out of the Secret Service, but you can't quite take the protect and serve out of a former Secret Service man."

"I think it's so romantic that he gave up his position with the Secret Service to come here for you," Jewel replied.

"Speaking of romance. I hear through the grapevine that you and Quinn have been seen around town, looking pretty cozy together."

It was impossible not to feel a stab of pain at his name. "Just friends," Jewel replied.

"Too bad. You two would have made a great couple."

Jewel took a sip of her tea then said, "I'm really not interested in being part of a couple right now."

"I highly recommend it," Georgie replied.

Jewel forced a laugh. "Why is it that every woman who has recently fallen in love thinks that every other woman on earth should be in the same state?"

"Because loving somebody makes you be more than what you were before you loved." Georgie paused to sip her tea, then continued. "Because loving is what we're made for, why we're on this earth." She gave Jewel a wide grin. "Loving somebody and riding horses, that's my idea of heaven."

This time Jewel's laughter was genuine. For the next few minutes the two talked about the Colton clan and everyone who would be at the barbecue the next day.

"Is Uncle Graham going to show up?" Jewel asked.

Georgia shrugged. "Who knows what Dad is going to do. He's really trying to turn his life around, but sometimes I wonder if it's a case of too little, too late. It would be nice if he and Uncle Joe could somehow put the past behind them and build a new relationship, kind of like what Ryder and Clay have done, but I'm not holding my breath for any miracles."

The two women visited for another half an hour, then Georgie stood. "I'd better get home, if you're sure there's nothing I can do to help with tomorrow."

"Pray for a break in this heat," Jewel said as she walked with Georgie to the front door.

"Isn't it terrible? I heard that a bunch of people were without electricity last night because of an overload of the system. Thankfully, the electric company got things back up and running in a couple of hours."

"I wouldn't even want to be a couple of hours without the air conditioner on days like these." Jewel opened the door. "Thanks for stopping by, Georgie. I really appreciate it."

"We all appreciate what you're doing tomorrow. It will be terrific to have so many of us in the same place at the same time. I'm really looking forward to it."

A few minutes later Jewel stood on the porch and watched as Georgie pulled away. She'd welcomed the distraction, but now it was time to get back to work.

The afternoon passed quickly and about five she started looking for the kids to return. She knew they'd be eager to share their day with her and hopefully they'd be exhausted enough to go to bed early. Tomorrow was going to be a big day for them all.

By six she decided to go ahead and eat something instead of waiting for everyone to return. Jeff and Cheryl had probably treated the kids to dinner in a roadside café.

As she ate leftover meat loaf with green beans and a salad, she thought of the conversation she'd shared with Georgie.

There had been a moment when she'd felt love for Quinn, when he'd filled her heart and soul and she'd never wanted to leave his arms. There had been an aching moment when she'd been brimming with the possibility of him…of them together, but with the possibility gone, she was left empty.

Once again the silence that surrounded her was suffocating. She couldn't wait for everyone to get back where they belonged, for the house to be over-flowing with lively chatter and laughter.

It's better this way, she thought, once again thinking of Quinn. Even if he hadn't been the one who had broken into the ranch, even if his limp really was from an old injury, she wasn't in a place to tie her life to somebody else's.

As long as she suffered from those haunting memories after midnight each night, as long as Andrew and the baby she'd lost cried out to her from the grave, called her from the woods, there was no place for another man in her life.

But if she were going to pick the man she'd want to spend her life with, it would be the Quinn Logan who had laughed with the kids in the pasture on the day of the picnic. It would be the Quinn who had made love to her with a gentleness and a passion that had her believing in happy-ever-afters.

And tomorrow she'd have to see him and socialize with him and wonder if he was some sort of psycho stalker or the man she should never have let slip through her fingers.

By seven, all thoughts of Quinn had disappeared as she stood at the front window and stared worriedly out at the road. They should have been home by now. She'd tried to call Cheryl's cell phone twice but each call had gone directly to voice mail.

She opened the front door and stepped out on the covered porch. The heat was like a sickening slap in her face. With the sun beginning to set, it should have cooled off, but the heat was as fierce now as it had been at noon. Not a breath of air stirred around her. It was even too hot for the insects to have begun their nightly hum and whirr.

Where were Jeff and Cheryl with the kids? The plan had been for them to be home for dinner. What could have happened and why wasn't Cheryl answering her phone?

It wasn't long before she felt it again…that disquieting sensation of being watched. She backed closer to the door and wrapped her arms around her shoulders, chilled despite the heat of the night.

Was there somebody out there?

Watching her?

Somebody who knew she was all alone?

Stop it, she mentally commanded. Those kinds of thoughts would only freak her out.

The sound of the ringing phone pulled her back inside and she raced to grab the receiver in the living room. It was Jeff.

"We've got a busted alternator and a dead cell phone," he said. "Don't worry. We're checked into a motel for the night and the local mechanic has promised me he'll have us back on the road by ten tomorrow morning."

Jewel breathed a sigh of relief. "What happened to the cell phone? Did you just forget to take the charger?"

"Actually, it kind of got crushed. We were stuck on the side of the road for a while. It was hot and Barry got nervous. He had a little meltdown and stepped on the phone. He's fine now," Jeff said hurriedly. "I've got insurance on the phone and everything is okay."

"I was getting so worried."

"I'm sorry. We just didn't have a way of calling until now."

"And you're sure the kids are okay?"

Jeff laughed. "They're calling it the big adventure and we're all in one room with roll-away beds wall to wall. We'll feed them a good breakfast in the morning and we should be there in plenty of time to get them cleaned up for the party."

"Keep all the receipts for everything and you'll be reimbursed," Jewel said.

"I'm not worried about it. We'll see you tomorrow and don't you worry. We have everything under control."

Jewel breathed a sigh of relief as she hung up the phone. Even though she'd known that Jeff and Cheryl would have things under control, she was grateful that everything was fine, that the bus would be fixed and they'd be home in the morning.

Now all she had to do was get through the night alone. Normally, she didn't mind time alone, but she'd been on edge all day and would have much preferred her "family" home with her where they belonged.

Exhausted from her day of work, she took a shower and got into her nightgown and robe. She carried a book into the family room and curled up on the sofa. She turned on a lamp as the darkness of nightfall encroached, stealing the light in the room.

She started to read, but the silence bothered her. She punched on the television and found an old movie that she'd seen several times before. She wasn't interested in watching it again, but welcomed the noise as she returned her attention to her book.

The lights and the television went off as the power failed. The abruptness of the power failure made her heart double-jump in her chest. For a long moment she remained unmoving in the darkness of the room.

Dark energy charged the air, as it often did before a terrible storm, but there were no storms forecasted, even though the area desperately needed some rain.

The heat, she thought as she got up from the sofa. Georgie had just mentioned that the power company was having problems because of the intense heat. There must be an overload of the system somewhere.

She turned off the television, not wanting the electricity to come back on in the middle of the night and wake her suddenly. She grabbed her book and went into her quarters.

The first thing she did was make her way through the darkness to her bathroom, where she had a stock of emergency candles on a shelf. She took out several, lit them and set them on the nightstand next to her bed, then with the candlelight creating flickering shadows on the walls, she got into bed and opened her book.

Abe Lincoln might have been able to read by candlelight, but Jewel found her mind wandering away from her book and back to the past.

The loneliness etched into her heart had existed long before the loss of Andrew and her baby, although that particular devastation had certainly deepened the wounds.

The loneliness had begun at a time when she'd been desperate to connect to her mother. When she'd been old enough to learn the truth about Patsy, all she'd wanted was to help the woman who had given her life, to find that bond of love that surely had to exist.

The need to help her mother was part of what had driven Jewel into psychology. The fact that she'd been too late to help Patsy had begun the hole of loneliness that gnawed inside her.

Quinn had filled that hole. Quinn had taken away her loneliness for a little while, until she'd seen that limp, until the trust she'd started to give to him had been destroyed.

She closed her eyes and tried to conjure up a picture of Andrew, for a moment surprised when the only man whose vision filled her head was Quinn.

Quinn with his beautiful topaz eyes.

Quinn with that wonderful mane of hair and the endearing habit of brushing it out of his eyes.

She squeezed her eyes more tightly closed. She didn't want to think about him. There was no point in regretting what would never be.

She'd rather think of that moment of sheer happiness in the restaurant with Andrew, when he'd placed the ring on her finger and she'd rubbed her hand across the place where his baby grew inside her.

Tears stung her eyes. God, she'd wanted to be a mother. She'd wanted the scent of baby powder and formula, the sound of baby coos and the joy of kissing a sweet belly as she changed diapers. She'd wanted that more than anything in her life.

Although she loved the children who were under her care at the ranch, she never lost sight that her job was to heal them and then send them back to their real lives and to their own mothers and fathers.

She opened her eyes and blew out the candles, knowing she wouldn't read anymore tonight. Hopefully, in the next couple of hours, the power would come back on, for already she felt the coolness of the air-conditioning vanishing beneath the weight of the heat outdoors.

Maybe she should crack a window open. It wouldn't take long before the house would be stifling. She crept from the bed and opened the window and that's when she heard it—the mournful cry of a newborn baby.

## Chapter 12

Something had changed.

Quinn saddled up Noches and while he sweet-talked the black stallion, his mind was filled with thoughts of Jewel.

Something had changed with her in the last week and he couldn't quite put his finger on it.

He knew she was busy with the preparations for Joe and Meredith's visit and the barbecue she'd planned, but what he sensed in her tone wasn't preoccupation with everything that was going on; rather, it was as if she were emotionally distancing herself from him.

She'd been pleasant enough, but there was an edge in her voice that cut through his heart, that definitely concerned him.

He'd thought about stopping in at her place when he'd driven by it a little earlier to go to Clay's, but as he'd passed he'd seen that all her lights were out and assumed everyone was already in bed. The last thing he wanted to do was disturb her if she was getting some much-needed sleep.

The moon overhead was nearly full, spilling down enough light that a nighttime ride had sounded appealing. Besides, concern about Jewel had kept sleep at bay the last couple of nights and he didn't think tonight would be any different.

Noches left the stable with a spirited shake of his head, as if eager to run despite the heat of the night. Quinn held the reins loosely, allowing the horse to lead the way across the moonlit landscape at a quick pace.

The night air made Quinn feel as if he wore a blanket around him even though he was clad only in jeans and a short-sleeved navy T-shirt. Noches didn't seem to mind the heat as he pranced energetically along the path that led to open pasture.

These night rides were Quinn's contemplation and relaxing time. After his wife's death and during those dark days when he'd felt as if the town had turned against him, riding in the evening had kept him sane.

All the aches of the day faded, all the disappointments that life had heaped on him melted away as he just enjoyed the simple pleasure of the motion of the horse beneath him.

But tonight was different. Thoughts of Jewel kept

him from finding the peace and relaxation he normally found on nights like this.

He thought he'd finally broken through to her, had gotten past the defenses she'd erected around her heart after Andrew's death and the tragic accident that had taken the baby she carried. Quinn had believed he finally had Jewel trusting him, believing that they had a future together, but now he wasn't so sure.

What she didn't know was that he was a man who didn't give up. He needed her in his life. He wanted her there. And he would do whatever it took convince her that it's where she belonged.

"No."

The word fell as a whisper from Jewel's lips as the baby's cries seemed to grow louder and heartbreakingly plaintive.

She clapped her hands over her ears. The sound made her dizzy and sick with fear. It pierced her very soul and made her want to both scream and hide in a closet where the sound couldn't find her.

Only a shaft of moonlight that danced in the window broke the profound darkness of the room. But in that moonlight she could see her bed with its rumpled sheets. She could see the book she had been reading flat down on the nightstand.

She was awake.

She wasn't dreaming the sound.

She was either crazy or the sound was real. She lowered her hands from her ears and cocked her head to one side, for the first time really focusing on the noise as unemotionally as possible.

So many nights she'd suffered through this, so many nights she'd curled up in her bed and consciously willed the sound away. She'd always assumed it was the cries of her dead baby haunting her from the beyond.

But what if it wasn't?

What if it was real?

Her mind whirled as she thought of the black-market baby ring Ryder had infiltrated a month before. Was it possible the baby she heard crying was real and not a figment of her imagination?

She stood at the window and stared out into the night, her muscles tensed and her heart pounding wildly. Always before, the sound had stopped as abruptly as it had started. She remained frozen, waiting, praying for it to end, but the sound continued…and continued.

She had to know the truth. She had to find the source. For the first time she recognized the possibility that it might not be in her mind, that she just might not be crazy. She acknowledged that the baby might be real.

Whirling away from the window, she stepped into her bedroom slippers and grabbed her bat, then opened the door that led outside.

She walked around the edge of the pool and to the back gate where she paused and cocked her head to listen. Nothing.

She couldn't hear the baby anymore. The heat wrapped around her, suffocating her, and the night offered an ominous silence, as if every insect and night creature held their breath in anticipation, but anticipation of what?

The hairs on her nape rose and a chill slivered up her spine. Her body tensed in alarm. She sensed something…somebody nearby.

"Jewel." The voice rode a breeze like a hot whisper.

She gasped and gripped the bat more tightly in her sweaty hand. Andrew. It had sounded like Andrew. Her mind felt sharper, clearer than it had in months.

It couldn't be Andrew. He was dead. But the voice was real. She felt it in her very bones. The voice was real and it wasn't Andrew's.

Somebody was stalking her, somebody was making her think it was her dead fiancé calling to her in the night. She couldn't imagine why anyone would do such a thing, couldn't imagine who might be responsible, but she was determined to find out.

"Jewel, come to me." The voice came again, low and hypnotic, but this time she steeled herself against it. She couldn't be sure where exactly it came from. The trees and brush played tricks with the sound, making it appear to come from all around her.

The moonlight momentarily disappeared as a cloud chased across the sky. She unfastened the gate and walked through it and onto the path that led to the Bar None. "Where are you?" She kept her voice soft and low as she walked deeper into the woods.

She sensed that she was not alone. Every tensed muscle in her body, every taut nerve she possessed told her that somebody else was in the woods, something who wanted her to believe that she was haunted by the dead.

She hadn't walked far on the path when she saw a figure ahead of her. She jumped off the path and hid behind a tree, her heart banging against her ribs.

Leaning around the tree, she looked at the figure and as the moonlight once again appeared, she recognized the tall man with the mane of hair.

Quinn.

She wanted to fall to her knees and weep. Only now did she realize a part of her had held out some hope that he truly was the man she'd wanted to believe he was, that he wasn't the person who had broken into the ranch and tried to hurt her. The pain that ripped through her as she stared at him on the shadowy path nearly destroyed her.

A hand fell on her shoulder and she screamed, but the scream was cut short as the same hand slid up and over her mouth. She half turned to see Adam. He indicated for her to keep quiet and removed his hand from her mouth.

"Follow me," he whispered. He grabbed her bat and tossed it aside. "You're safe now," he said, and took her by the hand.

She wanted to ask him what he was doing out here, but she didn't speak until they had gone some distance and she knew Quinn wouldn't be able to hear their voices.

"What are you doing out here, Adam?" she whispered.

He dropped her hand but continued to walk. "Since the night of the break-in I've been watching your place. I saw Logan skulking around and then I heard him call your name. I knew he was up to no good. Now, I need to show you something."

"What?" she asked, struggling to keep the tears at bay as she thought of Quinn.

He shook his head, his expression grim. "You have to see it to believe it."

Heart thudding in a combination of pain and apprehension, Jewel continued to follow Adam, wondering where on earth he was taking her. She could tell that they were on Bar None land, but they were headed to an area of the property where she'd never been before.

They finally broke out into a clearing where an old barn with gray weathered boards stood, listing precariously to one side. "You've got to see what's inside," Adam said.

The door opened with a creak of rusty hinges. A small work light hung from the rafter, creating a small pool of light inside.

The first thing Jewel saw was a tall pole embedded in the ground in the center of the barn. Around the bottom of the pole, brush and dry wood had been gathered.

"Oh my God, what is this place?" she asked.

She turned to look at Adam, his features taut and almost frightening in the dimness of the light and the play of shadows.

He drew his gun and smiled, his eyes gleaming with an ominous light. "This is the place where you'll pay for the sins of your mother."

Quinn had decided to go to Jewel's place and see if he could talk to her. The distance he'd felt from her over the past week gnawed at him and he wanted to talk to her before the barbecue the next day. He needed to make sure that things were okay between them.

He'd gotten halfway to her place when he'd hesitated. What if she were sleeping soundly, peacefully? Knowing that sleep was an issue for her, did he really want to wake her up, knowing that she had a full day ahead of her tomorrow?

He'd stopped on the path and that's when he heard it, a sharp, quick scream that sounded as if it had been cut short. He froze, all his senses on alert. There was only one woman he knew who often walked these woods at night and that was Jewel.

He raced down the path, his heart pounding as he looked left and right, afraid of what he might see, afraid of what he might not see.

Reaching the gate that led to the pool area of the Hopechest Ranch, he saw that it was open and beyond that the door that led into Jewel's private quarters was open, as well.

As he ran around the pool and to the door, he knew instinctively that she wouldn't be inside sleeping peacefully in her bed, not with the door open.

Still, he didn't slow his pace until he stood in the door leading into her bedroom and saw the empty bed. "Jewel?" he called softly, not wanting to awaken anyone else in the house. "Jewel, are you in here?"

He could smell her, that fresh floral scent that went right to his head. He flipped on the light switch next to the door, but nothing happened.

What the hell? He tried another light with the same result. He knew Clay's place wasn't without power and guessed that his place and this one would be on the same circuits, so why wasn't Jewel's electricity working?

This, coupled with the sound of that half scream had alarm bells shrieking inside his head. "Jewel," he called one last time although he knew in his gut she wasn't here. He ran back to the door and peered outside. She was out there someplace and what scared him more than anything was that something...or someone had made her scream.

"Adam, what are you talking about?" Jewel stared at him, then at the gun he held on her. She grappled to make sense of what was happening.

My God, was this somehow because she hadn't gone out with him? "I'm sorry if I've somehow hurt your feelings by not going on a date with you." This was Adam...Deputy Adam Rawlings. He was supposed to protect her. What was he doing holding a gun on her?

He laughed and the malevolence in the tone shot a shiver of icy terror through her. "Don't be stupid, Jewel. Do you really think this is because you wouldn't see a movie with me or share a meal?" The laughter faded and his features formed an expression of tense determination. "Turn around." He pulled a length of rope from his pocket.

"Adam, please, tell me why you're doing this. You said something about my mother? How do you know my mother?"

He motioned for her to turn around and, afraid of what he might do if she didn't comply, she did. He quickly tied her hands behind her back, then whirled her around to face him. His eyes were filled with the dark demons of rage.

"Why am I doing this? Because the Coltons have destroyed everything in my life." He grabbed hold of her bound hands and pulled her toward the upright pole. "Heard any babies crying in the night, Jewel? Has Andrew been calling to you from his grave?" He laughed and a new terror soared through Jewel.

"What do you know about Andrew? What do you know about my baby?" Oh God, this couldn't be happening. Her heart beat a rhythm of dread as she stared at him.

He smiled. "I know exactly what his face looked like right before I rammed into your car that night on the road. I saw his surprise, then his horror." His smile disappeared. "But it was supposed to be you behind the wheel. You were the one who was supposed to die that night."

Bile rose up in the back of her throat as she realized that this was the man who was responsible for Andrew's death, for the death of the baby who had never had a chance.

She struggled against the bonds that held her, wanting to get loose, wanting to kill him for what he'd done to her, to Andrew and to their baby.

But he held tight to her and roughly yanked her toward the pole with the dried brush and wood around the bottom, like a pyre for a witch.

He was going to burn her at the stake. The sudden knowledge shot a new wave of terror through her.

"Adam, please, don't do this. For God's sake, I don't understand. Tell me why you're doing this!" Tears blinded her as he forced her through the dry tinder and tied her to the upright pole. When he was finished tying her hands, he leaned down and tried to capture her legs.

She kicked her legs, trying to smash him in the face, at the same time screams ripped from her throat. He ignored her legs, and grabbed a handkerchief from his pocket and shoved it into her mouth. "Shut up," he screamed, the cords in his neck bulging out. "Just shut up."

Once again he reached down to grab her legs. She twisted and kicked, but to no avail as he managed to grab them and tie them to the pole. After trussing her, he leaned back on his haunches. "I haven't properly introduced myself. My name isn't Adam Rawlings. It's Adam Mayfair. Ellis Mayfair was my father. It's nice to officially meet you, sis, and let me tell you, I've got one hell of a reunion planned for all of you."

## Chapter 13

Quinn raced back down the path to where he'd tied up Noches, thankful for the bright moon overhead. The scream he'd thought he'd heard coupled with Jewel's open back door moved him quickly down the path.

When he reached his horse, he dug into his saddlebag and pulled out his cell phone. He had no idea what had happened to Jewel, no real evidence that anything bad had occurred except his gut instinct, and his gut instinct was screaming with alarm.

As he'd run back to his horse he'd searched the path where Jewel usually walked on the nights she couldn't sleep and she was nowhere to be found. He'd called her name out over and over again, but had gotten no reply. If she were out here, she would have

answered. If she'd just been out walking, she would
have made her presence known…unless she couldn't.

He couldn't get that half scream out of his mind.
If it hadn't been Jewel, then who would it have been?
And where in hell was Jewel?

He punched in the number for Jericho Yates at the
sheriff's office, knowing he might be raising an alarm
for nothing, but he'd rather be made to look like an
anxious fool than do nothing at all.

Yates answered on the second ring.

"Jericho, it's Quinn Logan. Look, I might be over-
reacting here but I just walked by Jewel's place. Her
back door was open and the gate leading to the woods
was open, as well, but she's noplace to be found. The
house is dark and I think the electricity isn't working
and I thought I heard a scream coming from the
woods a few minutes ago."

"Whoa, slow down," Jericho exclaimed. Quinn
drew a breath and started again, this time more
slowly even though each and every second that
passed filled him with agony.

"I'll head out now and see if I can figure out
what's going on," Jericho said. "In the meantime if
you find her and everything is all right, call me back
on the cell." He gave Quinn the number, who quickly
memorized it.

As he ended the call, Quinn remounted Noches.
He intended to search the property until he found her.
She needed him.

And he needed her. It had taken him five long

years to find a woman he wanted to spend the rest of his life with, and he knew without question that woman was Jewel.

But she was in trouble. He felt it in his heart, in his very soul. She was in danger and unless he found her, for the second time in his life he'd lose the woman that he loved.

Quinn knew there were three hundred acres of Bar None ranch land and he wouldn't rest until he and Noches had covered every square mile in an effort to find Jewel.

Quinn. His name roared through Jewel's head. She'd thought it was him who had tormented her, who had broken into the ranch. She hadn't trusted him, had been afraid to trust him. But he'd been the one man she should have trusted, the one man she should have believed in.

Adam told her that it had been him who had broken into her house, him who had gaslighted her with a recording of a baby crying and by whispering her name on the nights she went out walking.

And all Jewel could think about was that she'd never get the opportunity to love Quinn the way she wanted to, she'd never be able to accept the love he had for her. She'd been such a fool. She'd refused to listen to her heart and what it had been trying to tell her.

He'd been right. She'd been trapped by the same emotions Kelsey suffered, afraid to reach out for happiness, afraid that it might be snatched away. That fear had kept her from seeing the truth, that Quinn was exactly the man she wanted in her life.

And now it was too late.

"Your mother stole my father from me," Adam railed, once again the cords in his neck standing out with his rage. "And if that wasn't enough Joe Colton has managed to destroy everything that was ever important to me."

Jewel stared at him, unsure what he was talking about. Adam saw the puzzled look on her face and it only seemed to increase his anger.

"I had a cushy life in Reno. I worked as a security guard and one night I saved the life of the owner. Lola Justice was so grateful, she took me in, set me up in high style, then Joe Colton's newspaper the *Register* broke a story about her embezzling from the casino and ruined it all."

He paced back and forth in front of her as she desperately worked to try to loosen the rope that tied her to the pole. "Then I met Rebecca. She was nothing but a barmaid, but she loved me. You remember the story, don't you? I set her up in Georgie's house while Georgie was out of town. We took everything Georgie had and used a computer to start a hate campaign against Joe Colton. But Colton sent Nick Sheffield to check it out and Rebecca ended up dead. Everything…Joe Colton and your mother have destroyed everything in my life."

Tears raced down Jewel's cheeks and she tried to stop the sobs that wanted, that needed to be released, afraid that if she allowed them out, she'd choke to death on his handkerchief.

Half of what he said she didn't understand and certainly wasn't responsible for, but his hatred had obviously festered for years, an irrational, all-consuming hatred of her and the entire Colton family.

Her eyes widened in horror as he pulled a book of matches from his pocket.

*No!* She screamed the word over and over again in her head. *No! No!* She didn't want to burn to death. The very idea of dying by fire horrified her.

He pulled off one of the matches and lit it, then laughed as she struggled against the ropes, choking as she attempted to scream around her gag.

He blew out the match, then pulled off another, obviously enjoying tormenting her. "Tonight you'll pay for the sins of your mother and tomorrow I have a little surprise ready for Joe Colton. He won't be making it to the White House. Hell, he won't even see next Monday morning. It was nice meeting you, baby sister." He threw her a mock kiss.

Once again he lit the match, only this time he tossed it at the dry brush at her feet. For a moment nothing happened, then smoke began to swirl up in the air.

"Nice knowing you, sis," Adam said, and then he disappeared out the barn door.

A thousand thoughts shot through Jewel's head. She hadn't been losing her mind. Adam had been be-hind the voice that called to her in the night, the baby cries that had ripped at her soul. She wasn't crazy like her mother. Adam had been playing with her head.

As she thought of those nights when she'd been haunted by what she'd thought was Andrew's voice, when she'd been certain it was the baby she'd never had who cried out to her, she wanted to weep. All the doubts, all the worries that she was losing her mind—they had all been the responsibility of one hate-filled man.

The smoke drifting up from her feet grew blacker. The barn door that Adam had left open allowed in a faint night breeze and with a crackle some of the brush on the outer edges of the pile burst into flames.

A horror she'd never known suffused her. She was going to die here. The heat from the flames began to toast her feet and the smoke burned her eyes. Choking, she was racked by coughs and managed to dislodge the gag he'd shoved in her mouth.

Her screams were a combination of coughs and sobs as the flames at her feet grew hotter and bigger.

It wasn't enough that she would die here. Adam intended to kill Joe. Somehow he'd make sure that Joe never left Esperanza alive and there was nothing she could do to stop this vicious, malicious man.

Quinn. He would be her final regret. He'd told her she could trust him, but she hadn't believed him and now she was going to die because she'd trusted the wrong man.

*I'm sorry, Quinn. I'm so sorry.* She would die

with her regret, with the knowledge that she might have found her happy-ever-after with him.

A new spasm of coughing gripped her, leaving her lightheaded. Her chest ached and her throat burned as she continued to struggle to get free, but Adam had done a good job in making sure she couldn't escape.

She closed her eyes, hoping the smoke killed her long before she felt the burn of the flames. A weary resignation consumed her as the smoke filled the barn and the flames at her feet edged closer to the pole where she was tied.

Her eyes flew open as she heard the sound of a horse whinny. Quinn rode into the garage on Noches, who reared up, nostrils flared and eyes wide in fear at the sight of the fire.

As the stallion landed on all four legs once again, Quinn jumped off his back and Noches turned and ran out of the burning barn.

Jewel sobbed at the sight of Quinn. He raced to her and, stomping out the flames behind her, he managed to untie her feet, then her hands. He scooped her up in his arms and ran outside, into the hot night air, air that smelled amazingly sweet after the smoky interior of the barn.

When they were far enough from the barn not to be in danger, he placed her on the ground and cupped her face with his hands. "Are you all right?" He reached down and touched her slippers, as if to assure himself that her feet hadn't been burned.

"I'm okay," she replied, and coughed. "It was

Adam…Adam Rawlings, but his real name is Adam Mayfair. He's my brother, Quinn, and he tried to kill me. He's going to kill Joe. Tomorrow when they arrive in town." She was babbling and coughing at the same time. "We have to stop him. We can't let him hurt Joe."

"I know." Quinn pulled her against his chest and held her tight. "It's all right. He won't hurt anyone ever again."

She looked up at him and he continued. "I saw him sneaking away from the barn. He didn't belong here and I had a bad feeling about it, so I took him down. He's now handcuffed and tied to a tree."

They both turned to look as a whoosh went through the air and one side of the barn caught on fire. "We'd better call somebody," Jewel said.

"Jericho should be here any minute and I already asked him to call the fire department. Hopefully, they'll be here soon."

He helped her to her feet and once again pulled her into an embrace. "Oh God, Jewel, I thought I'd lost you forever."

"Quinn, I've been such a fool." She told him about the break-in at the ranch and believing that it had been him when he'd limped into the examining room. She also told him about thinking she was losing her mind, about how Adam had been gaslighting her.

She told him about the kids being gone and that it had been the sound of a baby crying that had pulled her from the empty house where Adam had been waiting for her. By the time she'd finished, Jericho had arrived along with a fire truck.

The rest of the night flew by as Jericho took statements and the firefighters kept the flames contained to the old structure that eventually collapsed in on itself.

Clay showed up and jokingly told Jewel that Adam had saved him the time and trouble of having the old barn taken down and carted away.

Adam Mayfair was led away by Jericho. He didn't say a word to anyone, but his eyes burned with his hatred for them all. He'd be jailed and would be facing enough charges to keep him away for a very long time.

Dawn was just beginning to peek over the horizon as Jewel and Quinn left the area and began the long walk back to the Hopechest Ranch. They didn't speak as they walked, although Quinn held her hand firmly.

It was enough, his hand holding hers. She didn't need his words to know what was in his heart. She'd seen it in his eyes every time he'd looked at her through the long night. She'd felt it as she'd leaned against him, absorbing his strength and calm.

He loved her.

His love filled her up, warmed her in a way the hot night never could.

And she didn't have to look too deeply into her own heart to know that she was in love with him, as well. When they reached the Hopechest Ranch, they went in through the gate and to the back door where she turned and faced him.

"It's going to be a big day for you," he said.

She nodded. "The first thing I need to do is call an electrician. Adam must have cut some wires or done something last night to make sure the electricity stopped working and I'd be in the dark."

He reached out a hand and placed his palm on her cheek. "I can't believe how close I came to losing you."

She covered his hand with her own. "I'm sorry, Quinn. I should have known that I could trust you. My heart told me I could, but I refused to listen. The worst part of all was thinking that I was going crazy, that I'd end up like my mother, locked away in a mental ward. I didn't want that to be your future with me."

He dropped his hand and instead pulled her tight against him, so close she could feel the strong, steady beat of his heart against hers.

"Even knowing that might be someplace in the future, I'd take the time with you now," he said. "I'd grab on to the happiness we could find together and hold tight to it, build memories of it and those would sustain me when things got rough. That's what I want, Jewel." His eyes flamed with emotion. "You're the woman I've been waiting for, the one I want to spend my life with. I love you, Jewel."

She'd told herself she didn't need the words, but they soared through her, bringing with them a joy that filled her up. "I love you, too, Quinn."

He leaned down and took her mouth with his in a kiss that emphasized the words he'd just said, a kiss that held all the emotion in his heart. And she kissed him back with that same emotion, with all the love and passion she felt for him.

She'd been searching a long time for the place where she truly belonged and she realized now that the place was in Quinn's arms.

When the kiss ended, he reluctantly let her go. "Is there anything I can do to help you with today?"

"No, it's all under control," she replied.

"Then I guess I should go and let you get some sleep or whatever."

She didn't want him to go. She felt as if she'd waited an eternity for her life to really begin and now with her love for him burning bright in her heart, she didn't want to put off starting to build memories.

"You know, Jeff and Cheryl and the kids won't be home until around ten," she said. "You could come in and help me with…whatever."

He grinned, a slow, sexy smile that shot straight through to her heart. "Why, Miss Jewel, I thought you would never ask."

# *Epilogue*

Meredith Colton sat on one of the lawn chairs next to the house beneath the huge tent that had been erected for the day's activities. The tent was packed with people and for a moment she was grateful that everyone seemed to have forgotten her, giving her a chance to just breathe and to sit and observe.

In the months since Joe had thrown his hat into the ring for the presidency, there had been little time for herself, but she'd supported him every step of the way. He had a vision of hope, of prosperity that the country desperately needed.

She gazed into the crowd, seeking her husband. She spied him in a group of men, his handsome face animated as he talked. Her heart swelled. Even after all these years the mere sight of him could make her pulse beat faster.

He would be the next president. There was no doubt in her mind, nor were there any doubts in the minds of Washington's most popular pundits. Short of a personal catastrophe, come January he would be sworn in as the new president of the United States.

A shiver raced up her spine as she thought of the catastrophe that had nearly occurred. Jewel had filled them in on everything that had happened the night before. Adam Mayfair had intended to somehow find a way to kill Joe during the barbecue today.

Meredith's thoughts drifted to her sister, Patsy. Patsy had spent much of her life trying to hurt Meredith and it appeared that her legacy of hatred had lived on after her death in the form of her son. But Adam was in jail now and hopefully that was the end of Patsy's reign of terror.

As always, when Meredith thought of her sister, conflicting emotions roared through her. She felt bad that no matter how many times she'd reached out a hand to her twin sister, instead of gripping it and holding tight, Patsy had bitten it.

A hand touched her shoulder and she turned her head to see Georgie. "You need anything? Want some food, something to drink?"

Meredith smiled and shoved away her sad memories of the sister she'd never really known. "No, thanks. I'm fine."

"I'm better than fine," Georgie exclaimed, her eyes shining brightly. "Nick just had a talk with Jericho. With Adam's arrest, Jericho has a deputy vacancy to fill. It looks like Nick is going to get his wish and be part of law enforcement here in Esperanza."

"That's wonderful. I'm so happy for you both," Meredith exclaimed.

"Uh-oh, I see Emmie bending the ear of one of the servers. I'd better go rescue him."

Meredith laughed as Georgie hurried away. Little Emmie had been charming the crowd all evening as she enthusiastically shared stories of school and new friends.

She wasn't the only little person charming the crowd. Jewel's children had been well-behaved and equally charming as they mingled and tried to help out where they could.

A new warmth filled Meredith, the warmth of happiness for her family. Clay had found his happiness with Tamara and Ryder had become the man they all knew he could be in loving Ana.

All of their children had come to the party and the tent was filled to the brim with Coltons and their families.

Jewel approached Meredith with a smile and a glass of iced tea. "I thought maybe you could use this," she said as she handed Meredith the cold drink.

"Thank you, dear." Meredith patted the empty chair next to her. "Sit for just a minute."

Jewel sat and Meredith reached for one of her

hands. "I can't help but notice that the attractive veterinarian hasn't been able to take his eyes off you."

Jewel's cheeks flushed pink and her eyes shone so brightly Meredith felt the sparkle in her own heart. Oh, she knew that look, it was the one she saw in her own mirror when she thought of her Joe.

"He's wonderful, isn't he?" Jewel exclaimed.

"He makes you happy." It was a statement rather than a question. If it had been a question, the answer was on Jewel's face. Meredith squeezed her hand. "I'm so happy for you, honey."

She'd worried about Jewel, who had suffered such a tragedy when she'd lost Andrew and her baby. When she'd sent her here to Esperanza, it was with the hope that she would heal, and it seemed that she had. The shadows that had darkened Jewel's eyes the last time Meredith had seen her were gone, replaced with the shining light of a woman in love.

They visited for a few more minutes, then Jewel left her to tend to some of the other guests. Meredith smiled as she saw Quinn reach Jewel's side and give her a quick kiss on the forehead.

The two of them were going to be just fine, and Meredith was grateful that Jewel had finally found what she'd been searching for, the love and support of a good man.

Once again Meredith glanced around and spied Graham standing just inside the tent opening. He stood alone, backed against the tent as if unsure of his welcome. His blond hair had gone almost completely gray and he looked sad.

Meredith knew her husband's brother lived in a big house in Prosperino and she suspected that the empty house rang with the hollowness of his life.

Graham had made decisions that had long ago driven his brother from his life, and after that, his children. Meredith had heard that he'd been reaching out to Ryder, Clay and Georgie, attempting to make amends for his poor choices and his absence during their formative years.

Meredith glanced over to where her husband stood and she saw the precise moment he spied Graham. Joe's back stiffened and for a long moment the two men stared at each other from across the room.

*Go to him, Joe.* She consciously willed her husband to move across the room, to go to the brother she knew he loved, a brother who looked hungry to belong.

*Go to him.* The past was gone and couldn't be fixed. All they had was the future. She didn't realize she was holding her breath until Joe began to walk to where Graham stood. It was only then that she released a sigh.

She watched as the two men talked and when Joe held out a hand to Graham and Graham grasped it with a smile, Meredith felt a wave of peace sweep through her. It might just be a handshake, but it was a beginning.

Meredith knew that she and Joe were about to embark on the biggest adventure of their lives. Joe would be the next president of the United States and she would be the first lady.

It would be a time of dreams realized, not just for herself and Joe, but hopefully for the nation. There would be successes and failures, laughter and tears, but she wasn't worried about it. The Coltons were survivors and whatever the future held, they'd see it through.

Tonight was about family and friends. It was about embracing this shining moment of happiness that filled her heart and soul. She and Joe would survive and grow with their love for each other and the love of their family to sustain them.

* * * * *

*Harlequin is 60 years old,*
*and Harlequin Blaze is celebrating!*
*After all, a lot can happen in 60 years,*
*or 60 minutes…or 60 seconds!*
*Find out what's going down in Blaze's*
*heart-stopping new miniseries,*
FROM 0 TO 60!
*Getting from "Hello" to "How was it?"*
*can happen fast….*

*Here's a sneak peek of the first book,*
A LONG, HARD RIDE
*by Alison Kent.*
*Available March 2009.*

"Is that for me?" Trey asked.

Cardin Worth cocked her head to the side and considered how much better the day already seemed. "Good morning to you, too."

When she didn't hold out the second cup of coffee for him to take, he came closer. She sipped from her heavy white mug, hiding her grin and her giddy rush of nerves behind it.

But when he stopped in front of her, she made the mistake of lowering her gaze from his face to the exposed strip of his chest. It was either give him his cup of coffee or bury her nose against him and breathe in. She remembered so clearly how he smelled. How he tasted.

She gave him his coffee.

After taking a quick gulp, he smiled and said, "Good morning, Cardin. I hope the floor wasn't too hard for you."

The hardness of the floor hadn't been the problem. She shook her head. "Are you kidding? I slept like a baby, swaddled in my sleeping bag."

"In my sleeping bag, you mean."

If he wanted to get technical, yeah. "Thanks for the loaner. It made sleeping on the floor almost bearable." As had the warmth of his spooned body, she thought, then quickly changed the subject. "I saw you have a loaf of bread and some eggs. Would you like me to cook breakfast?"

He lowered his coffee mug slowly, his gaze as warm as the sun on her shoulders, as the ceramic heating her hands. "I didn't bring you out here to wait on me."

"You didn't bring me out here at all. I volunteered to come."

"To help me get ready for the race. Not to serve me."

"It's just breakfast, Trey. And coffee." Even if last night it had been more. Even if the way he was looking at her made her want to climb back into that sleeping bag. "I work much better when my stomach's not growling. I thought it might be the same for you."

"It is, but I'll cook. You made the coffee."

"That's because I can't work at all without caffeine."

"If I'd known that, I would've put on a pot as soon I got up."

"What time *did* you get up?" Judging by the sun's position, she swore it couldn't be any later than seven now. And, yeah, they'd agreed to start working at six.

"Maybe four?" he guessed, giving her a lazy smile.

"But it was almost two…" She let the sentence dangle, finishing the thought privately. She was quite sure he knew exactly what time they'd finally fallen asleep after he'd made love to her.

The question facing her now was where did this relationship—if you could even call it *that*—go from here?

\* \* \* \* \*

*Cardin and Trey are about to find out that*
*great sex is only the beginning....*
*Don't miss the fireworks!*
*Get ready for*
A LONG, HARD RIDE
*by Alison Kent.*
*Available March 2009,*
*wherever Blaze books are sold.*

# BRENDA JACKSON

## TALL, DARK...
## WESTMORELAND!

Olivia Jeffries got a taste of the wild
and reckless when she met a handsome
stranger at a masquerade ball. In the
morning she discovered her new lover
was Reginald Westmoreland, her father's
most-hated rival. Now Reggie will stop at
nothing to get Olivia back in his bed.

**Available March 2009
wherever books are sold.**

**Always Powerful, Passionate and Provocative.**

# REQUEST YOUR FREE BOOKS!

## 2 FREE NOVELS PLUS 2 FREE GIFTS!

Silhouette® Romantic

# SUSPENSE

### Sparked by Danger, Fueled by Passion!

SRS08R

# You're invited to join our Tell Harlequin Reader Panel!

By joining our new reader panel you will:

- Receive Harlequin® books—they are FREE and yours to keep with no obligation to purchase anything!
- Participate in fun online surveys
- Exchange opinions and ideas with women just like you
- Have a say in our new book ideas and help us publish the best in women's fiction

*In addition, you will have a chance to win great prizes and receive special gifts!*
*See Web site for details. Some conditions apply.*
*Space is limited.*

## To join, visit us at
## www.TellHarlequin.com.

# HARLEQUIN Romance®

This February the Harlequin® Romance series
will feature six Diamond Brides stories featuring
diamond proposals and gorgeous grooms.

## *Share your dream wedding proposal and you could WIN!*

The most romantic entry will win a diamond
necklace and will inspire a proposal in one of
our upcoming Diamond Grooms books in 2010.

In 100 words or less, tell us the most romantic
way that you dream of being proposed to.

For more information, and to enter
the Diamond Brides Proposal contest, please visit
**www.DiamondBridesProposal.com**

Or mail your entry to us at:

IN THE U.S.: 3010 Walden Ave., P.O. Box 9069, Buffalo, NY 14269-9069
IN CANADA: 225 Duncan Mill Road, Don Mills, ON M3B 3K9

◈ HARLEQUIN®

# INTRIGUE®

## SPECIAL OPS

# TEXAS

# COWBOY
# COMMANDO

### BY JOANNA WAYNE

When Linney Kingston's best friend dies in
a drowning accident one day after she told
Linney she was leaving her abusive husband,
Linney is convinced the husband killed her. Linney
goes to the one man she knows can help her, an
ex lover who she's never been able to forget—
Navy SEAL Cutter Martin. They will have to
work together to solve the mystery, but can
they leave their past behind them?

*Available March 2009 wherever you buy books.*

Romantic

# SUSPENSE

# COMING NEXT MONTH

## Available February 24, 2009

**#1551 THE RANCHER BODYGUARD—Carla Cassidy**
*Wild West Bodyguards*
Grace Covington's stepfather has been murdered, her teenage sister the
only suspect. Convinced of her sister's innocence, Grace turns to her
ex-boyfriend, attorney Charlie Black, to help her find the truth. Although
she's determined not to forgive his betrayal, the sexual tension instantly
returns as their investigation leads them into danger…and back into each
other's arms.

**#1552 CLAIMED BY THE SECRET AGENT—Lyn Stone**
*Special Ops*
COMPASS agent Grant Tyndal was supposed to be on a mission to
rescue a kidnapping victim, but Marie Beauclair doesn't need rescuing.
An undercover CIA operative, she's perfectly able to save herself. As they
work together to catch the kidnapper, will the high-intensity situations turn
their high-voltage passion into something more?

**#1553 SAFE BY HIS SIDE—Linda Conrad**
*The Safekeepers*
When someone begins stalking a child star, Ethan Ryan is the perfect
man to be her bodyguard. But the child's guardian, Blythe Cooper, wants
nothing to do with him. As the stalker closes in, sparks fly between Ethan
and Blythe, and they soon find their lives—and their hearts—at risk.

**#1554 SUSPECT LOVER—Stephanie Doyle**
They both wanted a family, so Caroline Sommerville and Dominic Santos
agreed to a marriage of convenience. Neither expected love—until it
happened. But when Dominic's business partner is murdered, he's the
prime suspect and goes on the run. Can Caroline trust this man who lied
about his past—the man she now calls her husband?